Crazy Jungle
(Leo & Pala)

DR. HAYTHAM RAGAB

DEDICATION

To my parents,
my greatest gratitude for your support - I owe you
everything.

To my wife, Nanis,
thank you for your encouragement - you are always
there to support me.

To my two daughters, Jomana and Lojine,
you are the flowers of my life.

into the water.

The golden rock fell slowly through the water.

Finally hitting the head of a giant electric catfish named Losalo. "Ouch!" Losalo screamed.

His barbels bristled, and he noticed the golden rock, now at the bottom of the lake. He swam towards it. "Che Diavolo è questo?!"

Losalo's nasal barbels touched the rock, and he went rigid. Sparks flew. "Ahhhhhhhhh!" Losalo screamed.

Golden rays spread slowly across Losalo's body. He wailed in pain.

5

A MAGIC SIP OF WATER

The sun rose over Golden Lake, which sat on the floor of the Great Rift Valley. Grassland surrounded it, with cliffs and picturesque ridges in the far horizon.

"We're far away, Pala. Are you sure you saw the birds flying from here?" Mela said, voice trembling.

Pala poked her head from a bush to look out at the lake. "Yes, I am. The quake has to come from here."

Mela's head joined her. They observed a fantastic nature. "Wow! It's awesome!" Mela said admiringly.

Mela followed Pala as she stepped out and approached the lake. Pala nudged her and pointed to thin cracks that ran through the ground and stopped at the water's edge. "These cracks run into the lake."

Mela looked. "But why didn't we sense the quake before it happened, know-it-all? Even the elephants didn't!!"

"When I was in Nairobi, I heard talk about... an artificial earthquake," Pala added.

Mela's mouth hanged open in confusion. "It's earthquake humans can make," Pala explained.

"You learned a lot of things in Nairobi, Pala. I wish I went too," Mela commented, miffed.

Pala knocked Mela's head with a hoof. "I doubt you would learn anything, Mela. You're not clever at all."

Mela bit at Pala's hoof, but Pala pulled away and laughed. "Well, at least I don't pretend to be a great scientist," Mela challenged. "You're just an impala!" she said, teasing.

Pala looked at the horizon. "One day, I'll be a heroine."

"One day, you'll be the food for a cheetah, a leopard," Mela mocked.

Pala moved closer to the lake. As she did...

She STEPPED ON THE MAGIC POWDER THAT PITTON DROPPED.

Pala leaned forward and took a sip of water. Mela stayed behind.

"Or maybe... a lion," Mela joked.

A ROAR. Mela and Pala looked up, terrified.

"Did you hear that, Mela?"

"It's a l-l-lion."

"Run!"

Squealing in fear, Pala and Mela leaped towards the jungle. As soon as they disappeared, Leo burst from the brush. He looked around, admiring the setting. Leo didn't know that someone was watching him.

Far, in Pitton's cave laboratory, Sett ROARED as he watched Leo on the surveillance monitor. Pitton appeared over his shoulder. "Aha! An old friend?"

Pitton looked at Sett's SNARL. "Or... an old enemy!"

On the monitor, Leo drank from the lake. Pitton smiled nastily and caressed Sett. "Don't worry, my son. This enemy of yours, he'll be dead in days, or maybe even *hours*."

Pitton and Sett watched Leo sitting back on his hind legs on the surveillance monitor, taking in the beauty.

A FROG CROAKED loudly nearby.

Leo was annoyed at the noise. He rose and trotted away.

In front of where he sat, the WATER RIPPLED. Two long barbels rose above its surface, followed by a pair of eyes.

6

LOVE AND ARROGANCE

In the evening, Venata was pacing in front of the sleeping pride. Her eyes lit up with relief as Leo emerged from the brush. "Leo! Are you alright?"

Leo looked at her sharply. She bowed respectfully. "I mean, my lord."

"What's wrong, Venata?"

"There was a violent earthquake in the jungle and—"

"Yes, I felt it. So what?"

Venata timidly dropped her eyes. "I was scared something might have happened to you."

Leo took a paw and moved her chin up to meet his gaze. "Fear has no place in a lion's life."

Leo turned to leave.

"And what about love?" Venata said tenderly.

Leo stopped. "Love is a sign of weakness, and a

king should not…"

"But I love you, Leo," Venata interrupted.

Venata eyes welled up with tears. Leo stared indifferently.

"Do you love me, Leo?"

Leo's gaze turned tender for a moment before his arrogance returned. He strode away. "Tomorrow we leave for our new home," he declared.

But suddenly Leo stopped and winced in pain. Venata hurried to his side. "Leo, what is wrong?"

Leo gritted his teeth, trying to straighten up. "I'm fine. Maybe I'm… a little tired. It was a long day."

Leo pressed a paw to his stomach, his jaw set in agony.

At this moment, Catu called out to Venata, "Mom!"

"Go and see what the boy needs!" Leo told Venata. "Don't worry. I am fine," he reassured her, softening.

Venata watched with worried eyes as Leo disappeared into the royal cave.

7

ONCE, AN IMPALA BEAT A LION

It was late evening when Pala and Mela returned to the Wooded Savanna. They peeked out from a shrub. The herd lazed about along the treeline.

"Do you see her!" Pala whispered.

Mela looked right then left. There was no sign of Aipa. "No!" Mela shouted.

Pala threw her front leg across Mela's mouth. "Lower your voice, stupid."

Pala creeped out of the shrub quietly. Mela imitated her. Suddenly, they heard Aipa's voice from behind.

"Where have you been, Pala?" Aipa said sternly.

Pala and Mela turned. Aipa glowered behind them.

"Mmm... I was —" Pala Stammered.

"We were at Golden Lake, Auntie Aipa," Mela answered stupidly.

Pala stepped on Mela's foot. "Ouch!" Mela screamed.

Aipa looked firmly into Pala's eyes. "And why did you go there?"

"I just wanted to know where yesterday's earthquake came from."

"And a lion was about to eat us," Mela declared.

Furious, Aipa closed her eyes. Pala glared at Mela. "But we ran," Mela added, confused.

"Pala! One day, your curiosity will kill you!" Aipa said.

"I'm sorry, Mom!"

"No apologies! From now on, you are not allowed to leave the herd for any reason. Understood?" Aipa ordered sternly.

Other impalas looked over. Pala stared down, embarrassed. "But Mom —"

Pala's cut off with a yelp of pain. She staggered forward, falling to the ground. Her hooves kicked at her belly.

"Pala!? Aipa said, worried.

"My stomach!!" Pala screamed painfully.

Pala moaned. Mela tried to laugh, but her voice was full of worry. "Maybe because you drank all that water at the lake..."

Aipa looked sternly at Mela, who stopped talking. Aipa caressed her daughter.

"Are you still angry with me, Mom?" Pala said through gritted teeth.

"No, my sweetie."

Aipa and Mela helped Pala lay under the acacia

tree.

"Is our destiny to be a prey, Mom?" Pala asked.

"Maybe... yes. But maybe no. Much of it is luck." Aipa answered startled. "Why are you asking?"

"When I heard the lion. I had the feeling that I'd be that lion's food today."

Pala looked at her raised hooves. Mela looked at hers too.

"I wish I had claws instead of these hooves! I would have been able to defend myself better," Pala said.

Aipa smiled tenderly and gave her daughter a lick. "I will tell you a story your grandma told me."

Pala and Mela ears were upright, a sign of interest.

"Once, an unjust lion lived in the forest. All the animals were afraid of that lion," Aipa said.

As her mother narrated, Pala stared up at the starry sky. In her mind, the stars sprang to life, forming a scene in motion. Animals appeared, approaching a vicious star-assembled lion and making offerings to him. The lion accepted and softened.

"ONE DAY, THE LOTTERY STRUCK A SMART FEMALE IMPALA," Aipa narrated.

Pala imagined that the star rearranged to depict an impala ambling to the lion's den. The lion appeared angry and rubbed his belly. As the impala from the story talked to the lion, Aipa said its speech, "I'm the animals' messenger to you. They sent me with another impala for your dinner. While walking, a big lion took the other impala. when I told him that she's your food, he said that he deserves this land, grass, water, and animals more than you. he insulted you, and I came quickly to tell you that."

In Pala's mind, the stars showed the lion tilted its head back to roar.

"The lion said with outrage: 'SHOW ME WHERE THIS LION IS!'" Aipa narrated.

Pala imagined that the star clusters illustrated the impala leading the lion to a vast waterhole. They stood on its edge, and the lion saw his reflection on the water's surface. He thought it was the other lion. He lunged into the water... and did not re-emerge.

THE STORY ENDED.

Pala looked impressed. Aipa smiled. Beside them, Mela slept soundly.

"Remember, Pala! Your power is here." Aipa knocked her front leg against Pala's head. "You got it, my sweetie?"

Mela suddenly snorted loudly, sending Aipa and Pala into a fit of laughter. Then, Aipa tenderly licked her daughter.

"Good night, my love!"

"Good night, Mom!"

Aipa turned to leave but stopped. "By the way, the impala from the story was your grandma!" Pala's jaw dropped. Aipa winked and bounded out of sight. Pala watched her go, then yawned. She closed her eyes.

8

THE TRANSFORMATION

Leo was sleeping in the royal cave. Suddenly, a golden light sparked at his tail. It gradually spread across his body. Leo's tail shortened and balled up. The fur disappeared, giving way to a fluffy rabbit's tail. His hind legs extended and became larger and longer than his front ones. His sharp claws disappeared. Leo snarled in his sleep, revealing fangs that shortened and flattened. His small incisors became longer like rabbit ones'. Leo's ears got longer and curvy like bunny ears.

At the same time, Pala slept soundly under an acacia tree. A similar gold ray spread over her. Pala's tail grew, golden fur blossomed on it. Pala's tail got longer and thicker with a black tassel at the end. It became a lion's tail. Her hooves grew pointy, and sharp talons burst out from the ends. Pala's molar teeth disappeared. Two large tusks shot out of Pala's mouth, from the top of her teeth. Pala's ears got shorter and rounded like lion's ears.

9

THE SHOCK

The next day, Leo sat up abruptly. But he was no longer the Leo that we once knew.

He was still the size of a lion, golden and covered in fur. But his front legs had no claws, and his hind legs were hunched and long. Bunny-shaped ears flopped down amid his mane.

He opened his mouth to ROAR. "Roar... Ie ie ie."

Leo still could roar, but he now had an audible bunny snort at the end of his roar.

Leo was surprised and jumped to his feet, but his longer hind legs unbalanced him, and he fell. He looked down at his legs in shock. "Ah! What the hell is this?!"

Venata's voice came from outside the royal cave. "Leo! Wake up! Breakfast is ready."

Venata entered. Leo faced away from her.

He stared at his claw-less front paws in shock.

"It was a great day. We hunted a big..." Venata said.

When she saw Leo's rounded fluffy tail, she froze.

Her eyes shined. She thought Leo was a giant rabbit.
" What big prey!" Venata whispered.

She pounced on Leo. He turned around to fend her off.

"What the hell you're doing, Venata?! Are you crazy?!"

Venata eyes landed on Leo's long, prominent incisors. His floppy ears, his bunny tail. She backed away in horror. "What are you...?"

"Are you crazy? I'm Leo!"

"How dare you pretend to be the king, you strange, ugly bunny?!"

Venata lunged for Leo's neck. He resisted, flipping Venata and gazing furiously in her face. "You have crossed all limits, Venata. I'm the king, and I'll punish you," Leo threatened, angry.

Venata stared into her husband's eyes and gasped. "Oh, my God! Leo?" she said, shocked.

Far in the Wooded Savanna, Pala opened her eyes to see a group of impalas staring down in shock. Mela trembled with fear.

"Look at her long tusks!" one impala gasped.

"And her sharp claws!" another impala said, astonished.

Pala was the same size and shape, but from her lips, tusks protruded. Her tail was long and thick, like a lion's tail, and her hooves had turned into paws with sharp nails.

Pala stared at the impalas in confusion. "What —"

"Monster! Ruuunn!" Mela screamed.

Mela and the impalas ran. Pala watched them go, astonished.

Aipa appeared. She leaped towards Pala and looked at her daughter in amazement.

"What's going on, Mom?!" Pala asked, astonished.

Aipa approached Pala.

"No, Auntie Aipa! Stay away! It's a monster. It may eat you!" Mela warned.

Aipa looked deeply into Pala's eyes. "Pala?!"

The impalas whispered. Pala brushed past her mother to chase after Mela. She caught up quickly.

"Mela, I'm Pala, your friend. Don't you know me?!"

Scared, Mela leaped away. The other impalas followed her. "No! You're not Pala. You're a monster!" Mela screamed.

"Monster! Monster!" the other impalas repeated.

Aipa came up beside Pala as the impalas chanted.

10

LEO IN TROUBLE

Venata tiptoed through a clearing beside the royal cave. She looked around carefully. "Nobody's here," she whispered. Leo poked his head out of a shrub. Then, he hopped out like a rabbit.

"Are you hungry?" Venata asked Leo.

Leo nodded. Venata disappeared, returning with a piece of meat. Leo tried to eat it, but his new teeth didn't chew it. "I can't eat!" he said, angry.

Leo threw away the piece of meat. He hopped towards the waterhole. Leo bent to take a drink, but his eyes widened at his reflection. "Who's this?!" he gasped. Leo opened his mouth, shocked at his front rabbit's incisors.

Suddenly, Catu bounced on Leo's fluffy tail. Venata carried Catu away. "Stop, Catu!" she said.

"Who's this huge bunny, Mom?! Is it our food Today?!"

Leo closed his eyes. He didn't turn to look at Catu.

"Didn't you hear your mother?! Stop!" Leo shouted.

Leo snarled, revealing his rabbit's incisors. Catu leaned over, trying to get a look at Leo's face. "Wow! What funny-looking teeth!"

"Go away!" Leo said, angry.

"How dare you speak to me in this way, funny bunny!?"

"Stop, Catu! He's... he's... your father," Venata said.

Catu froze. "My father is a strong king, not a weird bunny!"

Leo turned around sadly to fully face Catu. Venata swatted Catu with her paw. "Shut up, Catu. Your stupid voice will awake the other lionesses. Go now!" she ordered her son.

Catu hesitated. He looked between Leo and Venata.

"I said, go!" Venata shouted sternly.

Catu ambled away.

Leo collapsed, and his eyes welled up with tears. Venata's did, too.

Venata and Leo didn't know that Pitton and Sett watched them from behind a bush near the pride.

"Your old enemy is not a strong lion anymore. Now, you can have your revenge, son. Go!" Pitton laughed.

Sett ROARED, his eyes on fire.

Leo and Venata looked up at Sett's snarl. They exchanged a worried look.

11

THE DREAM... AGAIN

P ala stared, panicked, at her reflection in the water. Mela and the other impalas hovered at a distance.

Pala's eyes welled up. She leaped towards a far acacia. Her new tail swang to the side; its further weight was making her stumble. Aipa leaped toward her daughter and helped her stand. Pala continued toward the acacia and lay down, sobbing. Aipa lay beside Pala, giving her a loving nuzzle.

Pala suddenly looked up. SHE REMEMBERED THE DREAM. She saw herself in her new form in Nairobi, running with a bunny-lion hybrid. Pala FROWNED. She remembered the young Caucasian woman with black hair that was in her dream. The woman was looking down at her tenderly. The vision was out of focus.

Pala's eyes lit up. "The dream! Dr. Caren!" she whispered.

"What dream?! And who's Dr. Caren?!" Aipa

asked.

"She's the veterinary doctor who treated me in Nairobi."

Pala stood, determined. "I've to go to Nairobi and find her."

"What?!". Aipa leaped to her feet.

"I saw her in my dream. She was treating me."

"A dream?! Nairobi?! No, Pala. You won't go anywhere!"

"Don't be afraid! I know the way to Nairobi. Please, Mom. It's my last chance," Pala pleaded. "I promise, if I live, I'll be back," she added kindly.

Aipa turned around, flustered.

"Look at me," Pala said.

Pala bent down and tried to bite at some grass, but her fangs got in the way. "You see? I can't eat."

Pala bounced around unsteadily. Her tail's awkward weight made her stumble. "I can't run! I'll die in a few days, either because of hunger or between the fangs of the first predator I meet."

Aipa tearfully turned back to her daughter. "I'll protect you."

"Listen, mom! You have to let me leave. Maybe Dr. Caren can help me, as she did before. If not, at least, I'll have tried. And, I'll have seen more of the world..."

Pala looked directly into her mother's eyes. "I'd rather die as a heroine who fights for her life than live as a poor, ugly, rejected impala —"

"Seeing the world? Being a heroine!? That's all you care about it?! What about me? If you die, don't I have the right to be beside my only daughter in her... in her 1-last days? At least, give me the chance to be beside you," Aipa said with a broken voice.

Aipa sobbed. Pala bumped against her mom's head affectionately. "I'm sorry, Mom."

"You're so selfish. Listen to me, Pala! If you live, you'll live here. If you die, you'll die here, with your family," Aipa stated firmly.

"But Mom —"

"It's over!" Aipa strode away angrily, leaving a dejected Pala alone.

12

REVENGE DAY

The lionesses startled awake as Sett's roar ripped through the air. Cubs ducked behind rocks. Venata looked anxiously at Leo and pulled Catu closer.

Then --

Sett bounded into the clearing with an arrogant SNARL. He slank around Leo and Venata, eyeing Leo's tail with a smug grin. "Hello, Leo! It's been a long time since we last met."

"Did I know you?" Leo wondered.

"Camus and Alba? Do those names mean anything to you?"

Leo shook his head.

"Of course, not! How would a haughty king like you remember the names of all his victims!"

Leo and Venata exchanged a look.

Sett stalked around the pride theatrically and began to narrate. "Several years ago, a white lion couple came here with their little cub. They asked the king to host them. He expelled them.

"They were hungry. But the king refused to give them so much as a bone to feed their little cub. They were thirsty...

"But when they approached the waterhole, the king was on them in a flash. His paws hit the couple, hit teeth snap. The father was so wounded. He died after a few days. Two days later, the mother died of hunger. But... The cub lived."

Sett glared at Leo. "My name is Sett, and that cub is me. You killed my parents. Today I take revenge."

Leo was shocked. He tried to justify it. "Your father was an invader, and I had to protect my land and —"

"Invader?! How can two weak, homeless lions and a small cub be invaders?" Sett interrupted. "You killed my parents because they were a different color," he snarled.

Sett eyes welled up with tears. Venata stepped forward. "I'm so sorry, Sett —"

"No, no, my beautiful lady. You don't have to be sorry. For three reasons."

Sett turned to look Leo directly in the eye. "Do you know what hurts a selfish king most? Taking his kingdom."

Sett turned to Venata. "And you know what breaks an arrogant man? Taking his beautiful wife," he winked sinisterly.

Sett coldly turned to Catu, who trembled behind

Venata. "And making him watch while I kill his son."

Catu cowered. The other cubs sank into the grass.

The lionesses looked scared. Leo leaped between Sett and Venata.

Leo's lip curled, revealing his rabbit's incisors. "Over my dead body."

"I love your new teeth, Leo!" Sett mocked. "Please, show them again," he laughed.

Leo swiped at Sett, hitting him with his paw. Leo flipped Sett. "Run!" Leo shouted at Venata.

"I can't leave you —"

"Venata, The cubs!" Leo said sternly.

Leo flipped Sett, who SNARLED and hit him back. Venata looked between Leo and the cubs. "I said, go!" Leo shouted.

Venata bit the back of a young cub neck and bounded away while Catu and the other cubs followed. Angry, Sett stood up and tried to go after them, but Leo jumped on him and brought him down.

"I'll catch them later," Sett smiled. "Let's dance," he glared at Leo.

Leo and Sett stood before each other. Sett lunged. Leo tried to move quickly but fell because of his odd gait.

Sett raised a paw, his sharp claws extended. He raked his claws across Leo's face. "Does it hurt, Mr. Funny Bunny?!"

Sett held Leo down. "I remember I've seen this

before! You did this to my father. But now, you see... we've changed roles," he savored the moment.

Sett pressed on Leo's front legs. Leo screamed. "Roar... Ie ie ie-".

Leo threw dust in Sett's eyes and kicked him off. He stood on his feet immediately, hastily limping away.

Sett turned to the terrified lionesses with a ROAR. "Your king is a coward. He runs away! I'm your new king!"

The lionesses remained silent. Sett ROARED, baring sharp teeth. "Bow your heads!"

The lionesses trembled as they bowed. When they looked up, they began to GROWL. Sett turned to see that a terrified Pitton has emerged from the brush.

Sett bared his teeth at the lionesses, who backed off. "This is my father! Bow to welcome our guest!" Sett growled sternly.

The lionesses whispered among themselves, then slowly bowed. Sett and Pitton swaggered among them.

"The gold needs protection," Pitton muttered. "Like an army of lions," he smiled wildly.

13

ESCAPE

The moonlight spilled onto the Wooded Savanna. Pala opened her eyes and sat up while Aipa slept soundly beside her.

Pala watched her a moment, her eyes full of love. Tears fell down her face. She slowly stood and ran towards the wooded jungle.

Pala leaped unsteadily between giant, old trees. OWLS HOOTED overhead, and a snake crawled by at her feet.

Terrified, Pala looked around her. In the blue fog, the dead trees with their long leafless branches looked ghostly.

Pala felt lonely in a scary world. In her mind, she imagined her mother looking for her.

Far, on shrubland, Leo collapsed in the grass, licking his wounds. Suddenly, he heard a HYENA'S LAUGH. Leo turned to find a dozen HYENAS surrounding him menacingly. "Hee-hee-hee-hee-hee-hee-hee!"

Leo struggled to his feet. "Don't you know me?! I'm the king."

The hyenas looked dubiously at Leo's fluffy tail and his hind legs. Leo quivered with anger. He let out a ROAR. But it was cut off by — "Ie..ie..."

The hyenas exchanged smirks. They stalked toward Leo, laughing. Then, they leaped onto him.

A weak Leo swiped with his claw-less paws, sending the hyenas flying.

Leo ran for his life. The hyenas chased after him with glee.

Leo ran up against a waterfall's edge. The HYENAS' LAUGHTER was close. He looked down at the FAST-FLOWING WATER, then behind him as the hyenas emerged from the woods.

Leo jumped. The hyenas stopped. They looked at the water but saw no sign of him.

Leo broke the surface of the rushing river with a gasp. The RAPID STREAM swept him away. He grabbed an overhanging branch and used all his power to pull himself to the river bank.

Leo stumbled from the water. His knees buckled, and he fell to the ground in a faint.

14

PALA AND THE KING OF CATFISH

Pala arrived at the Golden Lake. She heavily panted as she looked at her reflection in the water. She stared curiously.

Suddenly, the WATER RIPPLED. Hundreds of long barbels emerged, followed by beady eyes. Pala stepped back in surprise. She hurried into the brush to hide.

Losalo's head appeared. His eyes were more prominent, and his pectoral and pelvic fins had turned into four legs; the back two were webbed. Colored patterns were covering his skin.

He appeared to look like some kind of small catfish-frog, with long, shining barbels and fins on his back and tail.

Vandella, Losalo's wife, followed him. She looked like her mate, but her barbels were dull. Around Losalo and Vandella, hundreds of weird CATFISH-FROGS with long, dull barbels emerged. They all started CROAKING. Pala watched them, stunned.

" Silenzioooo!" Losalo shouted.

The catfish-frogs stopped croaking. "We're in a real disaster, king. As we've become frogs, we can't stay underwater all the time," one catfish-frog complained to Losalo.

"We lost our homes," another catfish-frog lamented.

"We can't eat our favorite meals: crayfish, clams!" a third catfish-frog stated.

"And don't forget pigeon! It's my favorite," Losalo commented.

"At least, we can still eat mosquito," Vandella said.

"Mosquitoes don't fill me up —" a fourth catfish-frog grumbled.

"We'll die of hunger," a fifth catfish-frog screamed.

"We want to be catfish again," a sixth catfish-frog yelled. The catfish-frogs began to chant loudly. "Catfish again... catfish again."

"Don't worry, my dears," Vandella said, pointing to Losalo. "Our great king will find a way."

Losalo moved his barbels around, deep in thought.

"What will we do now, your majesty?" Vandella asked Losalo.

Losalo raised his barbels upwards in a dramatic way. "I know that this seems like a disaster! But as your great king, I'll help you go through this ordeal, as I always do!"

Vandella proudly applauded him with her fins.

"We trust you, your majesty! So you've got a plan?"

"Of course, Vandella, I've got a plan!" Losalo said, showboating.

"And? What is it?" one catfish asked. Vandella and the other catfish-frogs eagerly looked at Losalo.

"Ummm. The plan is... The plan is —" Losalo Stuttered.

At this moment, Losalo and the catfish-frogs heard Pala's voice coming from behind. "I've got a plan," Pala said.

Losalo, Vandella, and all the catfish-frogs turned to see Pala standing in the moonlight at the lake's edge.

"Who are you?" Losalo asked, stunned.

"I'm Pala! A female impala from the Wooded Savanna!"

"And why do you look so?!" Vandella questioned.

"Maybe for the same reason, you look like you do!" Pala answered.

Losalo approached Pala cautiously while his wife and subjects hanged back. "You said you have a plan?" Losalo asked.

Pala tried to look confident. "Going to Nairobi!"

"Why would we go there?" Losalo wondered.

"There's a doctor there who can help us," Pala explained.

"How do you know?" Losalo interrogated, suspicious.

"I saw it in a dream!"

Losalo and the catfish-frogs exchanged uneasy looks. "A dream?! A dream?!" the catfish-frogs muttered.

Pala cleared her throat. "I don't have time to waste! And don't think you do either. You can come with me and have a chance to save your people, or you die here," she firmly said to Losalo.

Losalo hesitated and turned to Vandella. The catfish-frogs muttered among themselves. "To Nairobi! To Nairobi!"

"Nairobi is far!" Vandella stated. "Do you know the way?" she asked Pala.

Pala nodded.

Vandella respectfully bowed before Losalo. "In the name of our people, I'm asking you, your majesty, to help this girl to save us all."

Losalo closed his eyes and raised his barbels to the sky. "My dear people, I think it's time to reveal my plan to you. I spent the whole last night preparing it," Losalo stated, cocky. "I'll travel to Nairobi, find the doctor, and save the jungle," he declared in an enthusiastic tone. "Even if it costs me my life," he added, with a faux sadness.

Losalo bowed to his wife and subject's applause and cheese.

Pala raised an eyebrow.

The catfish-frogs connected their barbels, producing electric sparks that lit the whole place.

"Let's go, signorina!" Losalo said to Pala.

"First, we've to find our third partner!" Pala stated.

"What partner?!" Losalo asked.

"It's... a lion!" Pala hesitated.

Losalo and Vandella's eyeballs bulged. "WHAT?!"

"He was in my dream!"

Losalo trembled as he approached Pala. "Hmmm! You know, signorina... I think I am not doing well today. Maybe, we can postpone our plan for tomorrow —" he whispered.

"You can do what you like. I'm going now," Pala said. She shouted to make the catfish-frogs hear. "Your king will stay here. He's a little scared today."

"No, no, no! I'm going! Of course, I am."

Pala smiled. Losalo looked tenderly at Vandella. "Wish me luck, my dear!"

"I'm so proud of you," Vandella gushed.

Losalo and Vandella shook their barbels, producing an electric spark. "Long live the king!" Vandella shouted.

"Long live the king!" the catfish-frogs chanted.

Losalo stood on his hind legs to wave goodbye. He then joined Pala. "Where will we find this lion?" Losalo asked.

"The lion pride," Pala replied, without looking at him.

Losalo's jaw dropped.

15

SEARCHING FOR LEO

Pala and Losalo reached the Lion pride by the morning. They crouched behind some bushes and watched Sett lounging before the lionesses, gnawing on a bone. The lionesses licked their lips hungrily, their eyes full of hatred.

Sett disrespectfully threw them a bone. There was a scuffle for it.

"You said the lion we're looking for has a lion's front paws and bunny hind legs?" Losalo whispered.

Pala nodded.

"So this isn't our lion," Losalo stated.

Under a tent a few meters away, Pitton kneeled beside an unconscious lioness. He stuck a needle into her side and drew a blood sample.

"And who is that man?" Losalo wondered.

Pala was confused. "Um —"

"Our lion is not here! So, where is he?" Losalo asked Pala.

"Maybe he was expelled by this white lion," Pala

guessed.

"Let's search somewhere else before somebody sees us."

Losalo backed away. He suddenly fell into a deep footprint. Pala looked at it with excitement.

"That's a lion footprint!" Pala exclaimed.

Losalo noticed a smaller footprint a meter away. "And there's a bunny one."

Pala eyed both sets. "The footprints are consecutive. Lion's one then bunny's one."

Pala stared at the footprints, her smile growing. "I think they'll guide us to our bunny lion."

"I've got an idea!" Losalo shouted.

"Lower your voice!" Pala whispered.

"If we follow these tracks, we may find our lion." Losalo applauded himself with his fins. "What a clever idea! Follow me!"

Losalo took off. Sighing, Pala leaped after him.

****

At the waterfall area, Leo was sleeping on the grass. HE WAS DREAMING. He saw himself standing with Catu in a broad savanna plain full of different animals in his dream. "Remember, son! We rule with fear," Leo was saying, glaring eyes.

While dreaming, Leo saw Venata. She was looking tenderly at him. Her eyes were full of tears. "I love you, Leo," she was saying.

Leo also saw Sett holding him down. "I'll kill you and your cubs. Then, I'll be the king," Sett was laughing.

Leo was still dreaming when he saw Venata, Catu, and the cubs standing in a desert. Suddenly, a sand storm whipped about his wife and kids as they were tiredly crossing the arid sand.

The troop was climbing up a steep dune hill. Suddenly, Catu slipped. "Mom, help me!" he was shouting. Venata was reaching for her son, but she fell too. Screams were filling the air.

LEO WOKE UP, TERRIFIED. "Catu! Venata!" he shouted. He tried to catch his breath. Suddenly, he heard some voices beside him.

Leo startled and looked to see Pala and Losalo staring at him from a short distance away.

"Is this him?" Losalo asked Pala.

Pala stared at Leo. She remembered the dream when she was running with Leo alongside her. "I think so," she replied.

Losalo stared at Leo's bunny ears. "Oh, my God! He looks so weird," he whispered to Pala.

Leo glared at Pala and Losalo. "Who are you?!"

Leo ROARED, but a squeaking cut it off– "Roar... Ie ie ie."

Pala and Losalo shook with nerves. "Did he roar or snort?" Losalo wondered, stunned.

"I think... both," Pala replied.

Nervous, Pala introduced herself to Leo. "I'm Pala,

a female impala from the Wooded Savanna!". "I mean I was," she added, embarrassed.

"And I'm Losalo, the king of catfish," he trembled.

Leo stared contemptuously at Losalo, who shrank back.

"I was!" Losalo said.

Leo indifferently turned around.

"We're here to help," Losalo said friendly.

Leo glared at him. "How dare you? A king doesn't need the help of a weird frog like you."

"A king?! Are you a king?!" Losalo asked, stunned.

"I'm Leo, king of the jungle!"

Losalo jumped to hide behind Pala.

"You're not anymore," Pala challenged.

"What did you say?"

"I said you're not a king anymore!"

"I think I've found my dinner today," Leo growled.

Leo licked his chops, advancing on Pala. She noticed his teeth. "I doubt you can."

Losalo closed his eyes nervously.

Leo swiped at Pala with his paw and fastened his jaws around her throat. But his teeth didn't do any damage. Leo released Pala and shuffled over to a corner. Pala sat up in relief, breathing heavily.

"I can help you!" Pala said.

"Go away!" Broken, Leo hunched over.

"Don't you want to get your kingdom back, your majesty?!" Losalo asked.

Leo raised his head. "How?!"

"Going to Nairobi. There's a doctor there who can help us," Pala declared.

"How can you be sure?" Leo interrogated.

"I saw it in a dream," Pala hesitated.

"A dream!" Leo mocked.

Pala approached him, pleading. "I saw you in my dream as you are now. We were together looking for this doctor."

Leo shook his head. "Go away."

Losalo jumped beside Pala with a wink. "Va bene, signorina! Let's go to the strong white lion we saw at the pride. I'm sure he'll help us."

Pala smiled wildly. She led Losalo away from Leo. "You mean the new king? He's so strong and handsome. Like a real king."

Leo lurched to his feet with a GROWL. "Wait!"

Pala and Losalo stopped without turning around.

"How will we get to Nairobi?" Leo questioned.

Pala and Losalo shared a smile. They turned to Leo.

"I know the way. Maasai Mara, I spent my childhood in Maasai Mara. Nairobi's not far from there," Pala explained enthusiastically.

Leo thought a moment then sighed deeply. "I'm coming." Leo pushed past Pala and Losalo and hopped off. Pala nudged Losalo as they followed. "Nice trick!" she whispered.

Losalo smiled arrogantly. "Only a king can convince a king."

16

A VULTURE ATTACK

It was afternoon. Pala walked behind a hopping Leo in a desert near Mount Kenya. Losalo jumped beside her.

"Nice hop, your majesty!" Losalo flattered Leo.

"Why do you keep calling him, your majesty? He's just a funny bunny lion," Pala asked Losalo, wondering.

"Today, sure. But maybe tomorrow, this lion will get his form and kingdom back."

"What a hypocrite!" Pala commented, scornful.

"Grazie mille, signorina."

Off Pala's confused look —

"I mean "Thanks a lot" in Italian," Losalo explained, showboating.

"Do you speak Italian?" Pala asked Losalo.

"Certo! I learned it since many Italian tourists visit the lake. I can teach you some words: 'Bella' means 'beautiful.' 'Sorry' is 'scusa.' 'Piacere di conoscerti' means 'Pleased to meet you,'" Losalo replied arrogantly.

Pala looked eager. But SUDDENLY…

A giant lappet-faced vulture swooped in. Its talons closed around Pala's back, and it pulled her into the air.

Leo turned at Pala's scream to see her lifted to the sky. Losalo lunged for her and grabbed her leg. Pala pulled him upwards with her.

The vulture soared towards Mount Kenya. Losalo's barbels wrapped around Pala claws with desperation. "Help! Help!" he screamed.

Down below, they could see Leo hopping after them.

Pala struggled against the vulture's claws. The vulture swooped close to a rocky peak, and Losalo's head banged against the rock.

As they got higher, the snow covered the cliffs.

Leo hopped-ran as fast as he could. Up ahead, he saw a glassy peak. The vulture lowered as if heading towards it.

Leo seized the opportunity. He kicked off the peak and launched several meters in the air. He swiped at the vulture, hitting him with his front paw and knocking him from the sky.

Pala and Losalo span towards the earth, hitting a steep incline. Pala scrambled, her claws dug into the facade, and she managed to hang on. Losalo still clung to her leg. Eyes wide, Leo watched dangling below him.

"Ahhhhhh!" Pala screamed.

"Oh, Mio Dio!" Losalo yelled.

With a heave, Pala pulled herself up to the cliff's edge. She struggled to haul herself to safety but was shocked to find herself face to face with Ceros, a young male black impala with lyre-shaped horns.

Ceros offered his front leg, and Pala grabbed it with her paws, allowing herself to be pulled to safety.

Pala lay down on the ground, out of breath. Ceros looked down at her with amazement.

"Thank you for saving my life," Pala said. "I'm Pala!" she added timidly.

Ceros looked stunned. At this moment, Bupha, a red-billed oxpecker, landed between Ceros' horns.

"An impala?! But why do you look so?! I'm sorry, I mean —" Ceros wondered.

"It's a long story," Pala replied, embarrassed.

Ceros stepped back. He accidentally stood on Losalo's barbel.

"I beg your pardon, signore. Get off!" Losalo shouted.

Ceros and Bupha looked down to see Losalo.

"And what is this?!" Bupha wondered, pointing to Losalo.

"He's a catfish. I mean..." Pala answered.

"Scusa, signorina. I'm the king of catfish," Losalo interrupted.

"And why does he look so?!" Ceros wondered.

"I think we'll have the time to tell you our story,"

Losalo stated, nervous. "But first... Get off my barbels!" he screamed.

Ceros stepped to the side. From a higher peak, they heard Leo screaming. "Come!"

Pala, Ceros, Bupha, and Losalo looked up to see Leo on a peak above them. Ceros and Bupha stared at him in shock.

"That's Leo, the king of the jungle," Pala stated.

Ceros and Bupha's eyes widened.

"It's a long story," Pala and Losalo said at the same time.

17

ON MOUNT KENYA

Leo stood on a peak of Mount Kenya. Pala, Losalo, Ceros, and Bupha lurked a short distance away. Mount Kenya loomed beneath them, and glaciers surrounded. Far below, forested slopes and surrounding plains folded out to the horizon.

Pala approached Leo. "Thank you for saving my life," she said to him gratefully.

"I was saving mine," Leo replied.

Pala was surprised.

"You said you know the way to that doctor in Nairobi," Leo said coldly. "Now, how will we get there?" he asked Pala.

"I knew the way we were going, but that vulture dropped us on Mount Kenya. Frankly, I don't know the way from Mount Kenya to Nairobi –"

"So, we're lost?!" Leo bellowed.

Losalo jumped between Leo and Pala. "Don't worry, your majesty. We'll find a way!"

Leo snarled at Losalo. "What way?!"

Losalo trembled and jumped away. Leo glared at Pala. "We're stuck on this mountain, thousands of meters far from the earth. We'll die of cold or starve to death. And then, we'll be lunch for that vulture and his friends –"

"Maybe not!" Ceros interrupted.

Leo and Pala turned to him.

"I know a shortcut to Maasai Mara," Ceros explained.

"I can lead us to Nairobi from there," Pala announced, relieved.

"When can we leave?" Leo asked Ceros.

"Tomorrow, by the dawn," Ceros answered.

Leo stared at him for a long moment. He nodded tightly and turned.

Pala watched Leo, hesitated. "By the way, I loved your pounce on the vulture. It was amazing!" she said to Leo.

"Thank you," he replied coldly, without turning. Pala snorted furiously and stormed off. Leo turned to watch her depart and slowly smiled.

18

DR. CAREN

It was evening in Nairobi. A cell phone rang on a coffee table in Dr. Caren's apartment, the young blonde-haired veterinarian from Pala's dream.

Dr. Caren picked up the phone. The name "Prof. Thomas Williams," her father, was on its screen.

"Hello, Dad!"

"Are you busy right now?" Dr. Caren heard Prof. Williams's voice demand.

"No –" she answered.

"Perfect. I'll come to you in thirty minutes," Prof. Williams said.

"Is something wrong, Dad?" Dr. Caren asked, worried.

"I'll tell you when I see you," Prof. Williams answered.

He hung up before Dr. Caren could respond.

Thirty minutes later, Dr. Caren's doorbell rang. She opened the door. She welcomed Prof. Williams with a smile. "Come in, Dad!"

Prof. Williams entered. He was in a 65s, a white man with gray hair, and he wore glasses.

Prof. Williams gave his daughter a hasty kiss in greeting, then strode past her and sat in an armchair. He was antsy.

"Do you need some coffee –" Dr. Caren asked Prof. Williams.

"No! No! Come and sit!"

Dr. Caren seemed worried. "What's up?"

"Heard the latest?"

"You mean the catfish disappearance?"

Prof. Williams adjusted his glasses. "You know, Caren. It's not only catfish."

"What do you mean, Dad?"

"Yesterday, some residents living near the jungle called me. They marked the spread of weird frogs with long barbels. They also noticed some animals behaving very strangely. Other animals look like monsters," Prof. Williams explained.

Dr. Caren looked shocked. "You know, Dad, local people, sometimes exaggerate. They probably mean weird-looking animals."

"Up till now, nobody understood what was happening," Prof. Williams stated.

"And you do?" Dr. Caren asked.

Prof. Williams leaned back. He lighted a pipe and

began to narrate.

"Twenty-five years ago, I had a researcher who was working on turning water into gold. He experimented on small lakes in tropical forests.

"But his experiments began to harm animals. Some died. Others had severe physical changes.

"When I figured it out, I fired him. Then, he disappeared, and I've never seen him again."

Dr. Caren listened attentively.

"I think it's him. I think it's Pitton," Prof. Williams said.

He sat up straight. "The government has tasked me with forming a research team. We need a vet. Are you in?"

Dr. Caren's eyes shined. "Of course, I'm in."

Prof. Williams smiled. "Perfect. Now, Caren. How do you assess the situation?"

Dr. Caren thought for a moment and began. "The disappearance of catfish is critical. Many families rely on it as a source of income and food. Also, catfish maintain the balance of nature. They consume mosquito eggs and protect us from many diseases, like malaria.

"If we add the phenomenon of deformation of other animals, this means that these animals may be unable to consume their regular diet. Some of them will try to change their diet.

"This will disrupt the food chain of the whole jungle. Prey can turn predators and vice versa."

Dr. Caren looked gravely at her father. "Briefly, the jungle will be a total mess. A whole way of life might be destroyed," she said.

"But why the animals didn't die right away?" Prof. Williams asked, shocked.

Dr. Caren seemed sorrowful. "If we're working on the hypothesis that Pitton added some mysterious chemical compound to the water. Maybe it wasn't poisonous.

"However, this compound creates morphological changes to the animals, which means that it will affect their bodies' functionality and cause their death, eventually."

"How much time do you think we have, Caren?" Prof. Williams asked, worried.

Dr. Caren anxiously shook her head. "I'm afraid we don't have much," she answered, "not more than forty-eight hours."

19

CRAZY'S EVERYWHERE

D r. Caren and Prof. Williams weren't exaggerating. The magical chemicals that Pitton poured in the Golden Lake were transforming animal after animal.

In a Kenyan village near the jungle, many African women waved their brooms at a terrified Vandella. Countless catfish-frogs were jumping around them. The villagers were chasing Vandella and her mates with sickles, shovels, and spades.

In the Wooded Savanna, Aipa, Mela, and the impalas leaped around wildly in the grass. They, too, had produced fangs, and their ears had shortened and rounded to resemble lions'. Their newly thick tails lashed about. They were trying to graze, but their tusks were preventing them. They were hitting the ground with their clawed feet in pursuit of a slender cheetah.

In the Aberdare Forest, a herd of ELEPHANTS WAS GROWLING, shaking their heads emphatically. Thousands of strange parasites, resembling mini red-billed oxpeckers, were attached to the elephants' skin.

At Lake Nakuru, pink flamingos were hungrily chasing a rhinoceros.

In the Kakamega Forest, from high in the trees, black-and-white colobus MONKEYS WERE SHOUTING. They had long horns and red fearing eyes glittering in the night.

At the Samburu National Reserve, a fang-less leopard was eating a gastropod with disgust.

Briefly, the jungle was turning into a CRAZY WORLD.

20

WHAT'S REAL POWER?

awn had come. The sky was misty. WIND BLOWED. Clouds snagged on the cold peaks of Mount Kenya, releasing rain and snow.

Leo, Pala, and their comrades descended the mountain through a dense fog. Ceros led with Bupha on his horns. Pala leaped next to Ceros.

Leo and Losalo lagged. Nothing but snow and rock surrounded.

By the morning, the rising sun cast golden rays on Mount Kenya. Leo, Pala, and their comrades were still descending the mountain. Above them, a mother rock hyrax jumped on slippery rocks with her babies.

A rock hyrax male idled on a higher rock. He noticed Leo, Pala, and their comrades and called to his family. The mother rock hyrax and her babies hid in a hole.

Losalo made a big jump between two peaks.

By the late morning, Leo, Pala, and their comrades reached a Groundsels' trees area. They walked through giant trees about ten meters high. Cabbage groundsels gently unfolded their leaves and turned their faces to the sun.

Pala watched a sunbird land on a Giant Lobelia and fed on its nectar. "He's lucky. He lives away from our crazy jungle. Mr..." Pala said to Ceros. "I don't know your name yet!" she laughed.

Ceros smiled timidly. "I'm Ceros!" He pointed to Bupha, "and this is my friend Bupha."

"Who are you? Why do you live alone on the summit of Mount Kenya? Where is your family?" Pala asked Ceros.

Ceros looked dejected. He quickened his pace to walk ahead of the group. Bupha flew next to Pala's ears. "It's a sad story," Bupha whispered to her.

Pala looked moved. Bupha flew back and landed on Ceros' Horns.

By the afternoon, our friends reached the Dragon's Teeth area. Rainforest trees covered age-old hills. The Aberdares summits formed granite stones scattered in misty moorlands.

Leo, Pala, and their comrades walked through the stones, stopping at a small waterhole. "We'll rest here for a while," Ceros declared.

Leo, Pala, and their comrades drank thirstily. Ceros grazed while Bupha fed on his body. Losalo caught some mosquitoes with his barbels and swallowed them.

Then, the group lay near the water in the shadow of big stones. Leo sat with his back to the others, licking his body indifferently.

Pala stared admirably at the place. "You know, Ceros, you're fortunate. You travel all the time, discover new places. You also have your kingdom at the summit of Mount Kenya."

"A kingdom without family!" Ceros replied bitterly.

"Where's your family?" Losalo asked.

Ceros hesitated, but Bupha flew in front of him and nodded. Ceros sighed and began to narrate.

"I was born in open woodland in Kajiado county. When I came to life, my herd didn't welcome me because of my color. I didn't look like the others. Nobody played with me. I was rejected. Only my mother loved and protected me."

Leo stopped licking to listen. Ceros continued.

"But, when my mother died, the other impalas drove me out of my land. I tried to join other herds, but nobody accepted me. Finally, I decided to move far, far away. I chose the summit of Mount Kenya as a home, or maybe... an exile, with Bupha, my best friend," he tried to smile, "my only friend."

Bupha smiled, friendly at Ceros. Leo looked over his shoulder, a bit impressed.

Losalo closed his eyes and theatrically bent his head. Pala's eyes welled up with tears.

"Are you crying?" Ceros asked Pala.

Pala dried her tears. "I'm just thinking about my mom."

Ceros bumped head affectionately with her. "Believe me. You're so lucky to have a family."

Pala smiled. Leo looked on sadly.

"But what is the value of a family if you have no power to protect it?" Leo wondered.

"WHAT'S REAL POWER?" Pala questioned.

No one answered. Each of our friends started to think. After a while, Ceros began.

"I think love is real power. All love, not only the romantic kind," he replied.

"And you, Bupha?" Pala asked.

Bupha looked friendly at Ceros. "Real power is in friendship. My friendship with Ceros gave him the power to survive."

Ceros smiled. "Thank you, my friend."

"No. No. No, I disagree," Losalo croaked arrogantly, "power is knowing more than anyone else, so they needed you all the time."

"What about you, Pala?" Ceros asked.

"I thought that power is adventure, but now..." Pala sighed, "I'm not sure that's true," her eyes welled up with tears, "I miss my family more than anything."

Ceros smiled tenderly at Pala. He bumped against her head, affectionately.

They all looked at Leo. He hesitated. He took a deep breath and began.

"I had always believed that power is to make the others fear me," Leo sighed, "now, I'm wondering what real power is."

A moment of silence. Leo then retrieved his arrogance. He looked sternly at Ceros. "We don't have time to waste. Let's go."

Ceros nodded and leaped first in line. The group followed him.

21

TO MAASAI MARA

It was evening. Prof. Williams and Dr. Caren arrived in a Jeep at the Golden Lake. They hopped out.

Dr. Caren approached the lake and filled a test tube with water. She held it up to Prof. Williams.

"I took the sample, Prof. Williams," Dr. Caren said.

"Great, Caren. Let's go back to the lab. We've got a lot of work to do."

They jumped in the car and left.

****

The next morning, Leo, Pala, and their comrades arrived at shrubland near Maasai Mara. They weaved slowly through the trees.

Leo and Pala looked thin, and their movements were sluggish. According to Dr. Caren's estimate, they had LESS THAN 24 HOURS LEFT, OR

THEY WOULD STARVE.

Pala stopped suddenly and cried out excitedly. "I know this place. We're so close to Maasai Mara," she looked gratefully at Ceros, "thank you, Ceros! You're a great guide."

Ceros smiled timidly.

"Now, it's your turn, Pala. You said you know the way from Maasai Mara to Nairobi," Losalo stated.

"Yeah! But I've another idea. Many cars come to Maasai Mara from Nairobi. If we hide in one of them, it can take us to Nairobi quickly," Pala proposed.

"Sounds good," Losalo replied.

Leo looked suspicious. "And how will we get in this car, know-it-all?"

The others looked curiously at Pala as she thought.

"Some cars have a trunk. We can hide inside it," Pala suggested.

"And what if that car is not going to Nairobi? We'll get lost again, because of you. As always," Leo said.

"The vulture got us lost —" Pala defended.

"Hah! The vulture!" Leo mocked.

Pala angrily leaped towards Leo, getting close to his face. Ceros, Bupha, and Losalo stayed back.

"We're weak and starving. We can't walk anymore. We'll die before we get to Nairobi if we don't find a faster way," Pala said, angry.

"You said you had a plan, and you knew the way —" Leo replied.

"Yeah! I do."

"I thought you meant a good plan. Getting in a car! What if it's a hunter's car? They'll kill us before we reach Nairobi," Leo scoffed. "I've got a better idea. Why don't we drive a car to Nairobi?" he mocked.

Ceros and Bupha exchanged a look.

"What is a car?" Bupha whispered.

"I've no idea," Ceros answered.

Losalo overheard and shook his head. "Primitive beings!" he muttered.

Leo looked down at Pala. "You know, it's my fault. I should never have followed the dream of a stupid weird, ugly impala."

"Why do you mock me all the time? Who do you think you are, Mr. Funny Bunny?" Pala shouted at Leo, furious.

Ceros and Bupha's eyes widened. Losalo shifted nervously.

"Ouh, ouh!" Losalo muttered.

Leo GROWLED. Terrified, Losalo jumped behind a bush. Bupha hid between Ceros' horns.

But, our friends didn't know that two AFRICAN GUNMEN were hiding behind some shrubs, watching them. The first pointed to Ceros. "Look at that beautiful, black impala."

"What a great catch!" the second gunman replied.

The first gunman raised his rifle.

Back to our friends...

Leo was snarling at Pala. "Killing you will be the

last thing I do."

Pala flinched but stood her ground. "I'm not afraid of you!"

Leo advanced on Pala. She defiantly looked back at him. Suddenly, Leo stopped. His bunny ears pricked up and turned.

The ECHOING sound of a GUN LOADING was amplified.

"Get down!" Leo shouted on his comrades.

Leo, Pala, Ceros dropped. Losalo jumped inside a bush. Bupha hid between Ceros' horns. BANG! A BULLET WHIZZED over Ceros' head.

"What is this?!" Ceros asked, terrified.

"I think it's a bullet," Pala answered.

"It passed just over my head," Ceros stated.

"A hunter is trying to snipe you," Pala said.

Ceros and Bupha were stunned.

"So, this bullet may hurt?!" Bupha asked.

"It kills," Pala replied.

Ceros and Bupha looked terrified. Bupha flew upwards, spotting the two gunmen. "There are two humans there!" he whispered.

Leo crept low towards the shrubs. Through the brush, he saw the two gunmen a short distance away. "I see them. Stay here!"

Leo stealthily slank toward the gunmen. He heard them bickering.

"You missed it, idiot!" the second gunman was saying to the first.

"You see the animals with the impala? They looked so weird. They look like —"

A SNARL ripped through the air as Leo lunged on the first gunman. Leo flipped him over, and the man's eyes grew wide as he took in Leo's bizarre form.

"Monster! Monster!" the first gunman shouted.

The second gunman grabbed his gun, but Leo GROWLED. The gunman dropped his weapon and ran away. The first gunman stumbled to his feet and followed.

"Come on!" Leo called on his comrades. Pala and the others ran towards him.

"Vostra Maestà, let me express my admiration for your courage. You're so brave," Losalo said respectfully.

Exhausted, Leo lay down on the grass. Ceros bowed low with Bupha on his horns.

"Thank you! You saved my life," Ceros said to Leo.

Leo smiled tiredly. A few meters away, Pala noticed a Jeep hidden behind some bushes.

Leo, Pala, and their comrades jumped towards the car.

Pala and Losalo got in from the driver's window. Leo checked the back.

Ceros and Bupha looked astonishingly at the car.

"Is this what they call a car?" Ceros asked Leo.

22

CAR CHASE

P ala sat behind the wheel with Losalo in the passenger's seat. She held the steering with her front legs while using her hind legs to hit the brake and the gas pedal.

"This is one of my dreams!" Pala gushed gleefully.

"Holding this?!" Losalo asked Pala, pointing to the steering wheel.

"Driving a car! I saw many of them in Maasai Mara. They carried these annoying people who come to watch us," Pala checked the car, "but how does it work?"

In the back, Leo, Ceros, and Bupha sat among a plethora of guns and ammunition.

"What the hell is all this?!" Bupha asked, amazed.

"These are weapons! Maybe it's the hunters' car," Leo stared at the weapons, uneasy, "but what will they hunt with all these weapons? A whole jungle?!"

Losalo bounded around the car with excitement. He hit the HORN repeatedly, causing consecutive

BEEPS. "Yahooo! This is awesome."

"Losalo, stop! It's disconcerting!" Pala said.

"More than my frog voice?! Ak...Ak...Ak...Ak," Losalo joked.

"I said, stop!" Pala laughed.

Pala hit Losalo amiably with her front leg. He jerked back and yelped. One of his barbels stuck in the car's ignition.

" Help! Help! I'm stuck!" Losalo screamed.

Pala pulled on Losalo, but in vain. He panicked, and his barbel let out an electric spark. The CAR STARTED.

"What's going on up there?" Leo asked.

"I've no idea!" Pala replied.

"Get me off, Pala!" Losalo yelled.

"I'm trying," Pala checked the gear, "maybe this will stop the car."

Pala shifted the gear from "P" to "D." The car lurched.

Pala and her comrades heard the PURR of various ENGINES. Two motorcycles and three Jeeps full of AFRICAN GUNMEN appeared. Among them, the two gunmen who fled from Leo looked out the windshield of the lead car.

The Driver of the front gunmen's car squinted, seeing the animal's Jeep moving through the trees. "Who's driving our car?!" he shouted, "Kuacha! Kuacha!"

Pala's car continued moving. It burst out of the

jungle path and onto the road in front of the gunmen.

"Stop the car! Shoot on it!" the driver ordered his mates.

One of the two gunmen who fled from Leo leaned out of the window. He SHOOTED at Pala's rear tires but missed. The other gunman noticed Leo and Ceros in Pala's car's trunk. "There's the monster who attacked us! And the black impala is there too! What are they doing in a trunk?!" he wondered.

"Shoot them," the driver shouted.

The second gunman leaned out the car's window and SHOOTED.

The BULLET WHIZZED between Leo's ears, just missing his head. He looked scared.

Ceros and Bupha were terrified.

"What was that?! Bupha asked.

"It seems like the thing that flew over my head earlier. Maybe this is what they call a bullet?" Ceros guessed.

Bupha hid between Ceros' horns.

"Faster, they're trying to kill us!" Leo shouted to Pala.

"I'm trying!" Pala said.

Losalo's barbel was still jammed in the ignition. He struggled to pull it out.

The Jeep barrelled onto a forest road at full speed. The gunmen's jeeps and motorcycles chased them, FIRING.

Leo and Ceros ducked amid the loud

GUNSHOTS. Pala smiled as she drove and let out a — "Youppiii! This is amazing. I never imagined I'd drive a car in the jungle. I wish my mom could see me now. She would be proud of me."

"Duh!" Losalo commented.

Pala's smile disappeared as Losalo screamed. Up ahead, a vast rock sat in the road.

Pala looked at the steering wheel in a panic. "These usually change direction, but I don't know-how —"

"You mean like this?"

Losalo wrapped a free barbel around the steering wheel and yanked it. The Jeep teetered, heading towards a tree.

"No!" Pala shouted. She grabbed the wheel and pulled it to the other side.

The Jeep flung to the left, away from the tree. It speeded past the rock, narrowly missing it.

Behind Pala's Jeep, one of the motorcycles collided with the rock and EXPLODED.

"Yahooo! I did it! I'm great!" Losalo cheered.

"Great?! You almost made us crash!" Pala replied, stunned.

"Jealous!" Losalo muttered.

****

Pala's car got on a HIGHWAY. The gunmen were still after her.

The highway was a crowded two-way route. Many

cars and trucks were running on it.

Pala looked fearfully at the chaotic traffic. Her forelegs unsteadily navigated the Jeep onto the highway. "Oh my god!"

She began to veer abruptly between cars. Losalo swang from side to side, still unable to free his barbel.

"Ohhhh! I feel nauseous," Losalo panted, exhausted.

Pala looked in her rear-view mirror to see the gunmen's three cars and the remaining motorcycle swang into the lane behind her. GUNSHOTS flew.

Around her, the surrounding cars tried to veer out of the way. Drivers and passengers screamed as the gunmen ZOOMED by.

Pala jerked the wheel to avoid a car in front of her, but her front bumper clipped the car's rear.

A YOUNG BLACK GIRL peered out the back of the car. Her eyes widened as she saw Pala behind the wheel. "This is amazing!" the girl gasped.

She quickly pulled her cellphone out and snapped a shot. Pala's Jeep steered into a lane, swiping the side of a big truck. The TRUCK'S DRIVER yelled out the window.

"Hey! What the hell are you doing?!" he shouted.

The Truck Driver's jaw dropped when he saw Pala through the window as the Jeep whipped by. He turned to the passenger. "Did you see that?!" the truck driver asked, thunder-struck.

Pala kept driving, weaving through the traffic.

In shock, the Truck's Driver stared at the Jeep. Without realizing, he drifted into the lane next to him, cutting off the first gunmen's car.

The driver of the gunmen's car swang the wheel to avoid the truck and rammed into the highway-rail. The car flipped onto its side and came to a stop.

The two remaining Jeeps and motorcycle continued chasing Pala's car as the highway turned into a steep slope. Sandy hills surrounded the new terrain.

The gunmen leaned out of their Jeeps, SHOOTING at Leo, Ceros, and Bupha.

Leo ducked to avoid a bullet and accidentally stepped on a machine-gun on the car floor. It FIRED CARTRIDGES in rapid succession.

He watched in shock as the bullets peppered the front of one of the Jeeps. Its' WHEELS POPPED, and it flipped.

"Wow! Good shot!" Ceros commented, impressed.

Showboating, Leo smiled proudly. BANG! The animals dropped to the floor of the trunk. The last gunman's Jeep and the motorcycle were still in pursuit.

"We've got to stop them," Ceros stated, calling on Bupha, "I've got an idea. Let's go, my friend!"

In one flying leap, Ceros jumped out of the car. Bupha looked stunned for a moment but then flew out and landed on Ceros back.

The road became very sloping. Ceros sprang across the sandy hills beside the road. "I'll jump on the man with the gun. You'll deal with the rider," he said to Bupha.

"Are you sure we can do that?" Bupha asked Ceros, astonished.

Leo watched in horror as the motorcyclist pulled up alongside their Jeep. He raised his gun. Leo closed his eyes.

Out of nowhere, Ceros leaped through the air and rammed his horns into the gunman, knocking him off his bike. The man landed on the side of the highway.

Bupha was on the rider in an instant, pecking at his ears. "Oh! It hurts, my dear! Doesn't it?!" Bupha smiled.

The rider moaned and waved his arms in defense.

Bupha finally flew towards Ceros who was running alongside Pala's Jeep, trying to jump back in. Ceros leaped several times, but he missed the car.

Leo reached a paw out of the trunk. "Take my paw!"

Ceros bit down on Leo's paw, which pulled him into the car.

Ceros gasped for breath, looking up at Leo gratefully. "Thank you!"

Leo smiled. BANG! Leo turned to the road behind them, where the remaining car still followed them.

The animals swang to one side of the car as Pala

abruptly turned off the highway and into a trail.

****

They passed a small building at its entrance with a sign, "MASAI MARA NATIONAL RESERVE - OLOOLAIMUTIA GATE."

"Here we are! welcome my friends to Maasai Maraaaa," Pala rejoiced.

Losalo yanked at his barbel but still could not break free. His eyes widened at an iron gate that blocked the road ahead. But before he could scream --

CRASH! The Jeep shot through the gate at high speed, breaking it open.

The GUARDS operating the gate stood to take out their weapons, but the Jeep whizzed by with the gunman in pursuit.

"Hey! What are you doing?! Stop!" one guard shouted.

The guards ran for their Jeep and got in.

Pala's car got on Masai Mara National Reserve road. The gunmen's remaining car was still after her.

A gunman leaned out of their Jeep to FIRE his RIFLE at Pala. One bullet hit the car's bumper.

Ceros was terrified. He turned to Leo. "What now?"

"Save the last dance for me!" Leo replied, eyes glaring.

Ceros and Bupha exchanged an anxious look.

The Jeep zoomed towards a bridge.

Leo moved to the trunk's edge and launched himself into the air. He landed on the gunmen's windshield, blocking the driver's view.

Another gunman popped out of a window and pointed his gun at Leo. The king of the jungle punched him with his paw.

Ceros and Bupha watched in astonishment from the Jeep.

Leo crawled to the driver's side and SNARLED at the driver. Terrified, the driver turned the steering wheel and slammed the Jeep into the bridge barrier.

The car broke through, launching into the Mara River below.

Before it hit, Leo leaped from the car and landed back on the bridge. A few powerful strides, and he got into Pala's Jeep. He jumped into the back.

Ceros and Bupha stared at him in shock. Leo fell to the ground, exhausted and breathing heavily.

"Are we clear?!" Pala asked.

"I... think so," Ceros supposed.

"I did it!" Losalo chortled gleefully.

"We all did it!" Pala said.

"Leo did it," Ceros stated, still in awe.

"I love this teamwork spirit!" Bupha cheered.

"I hope this spirit rids me of *this*!" Losalo shouted, nervous.

Losalo pulled on his barbels as the others laughed

at him.

BANG! The Jeep lurched to the side as a tire went out.

"What the hell is this?" Pala shrieked, terrified.

Bupha looked back, seeing the guard Jeep chasing them. "The guards! Behind us!"

"Pala, hurry up!" Ceros shouted.

"I can't."

A big tree appeared in their path.

"We're going to crash! Nooooo!" Pala screamed.

Pala's car hit the tree hard. CRASH!

23

MARA RIVER

The guards' car stopped behind the wrecked vehicle. Its front was smoking, wrapped around the tree.

A guard stepped out of the car and raised his gun. "Give yourself up!"

There was no movement. Another guard followed him, and the two slowly approached.

The guard moved towards the driver's side window cautiously. "Put your guns down!"

He reached the window and pointed his gun inside. But...

No one was there.

The other guard checked the trunk, looking shocked as he noticed the weapons arsenal.

Not far, at the Mara River, herds of wildebeests, zebras, and gazelles were crossing the fast-flowing water. Steep banks lined either side.

Suddenly, a couple of barbels lift out of the water among the crossing herds, followed by Losalo's head.

"Ahhh! I'm free! I thought I'd spend the rest of my life stuck in the car hole!" Losalo gushed.

Pala and the others stepped into view, heading towards a bank among thousands of grazers. Bupha fluttered above.

"What now?!" Bupha asked.

"We'll cross the river among all these animals. The guards won't find us," Leo replied.

Losalo jumped into the water and then joyfully swang between wildebeests' backs. "Mamma mia! I miss this freshwater. What a feeling!"

Losalo landed on a rock in the middle of the river. But the stone began to move. It was a crocodile head.

Losalo shrieked. "No, no! Not a crocodile!"

The crocodile bared its teeth at Losalo.

"I'm just a frog! You don't like frogs! Do you? Ak...Ak...Ak..." Losalo trembled.

The crocodile opened his mouth, and Losalo jumped away. Leo, Pala, Ceros, and Bupha followed him. They finally arrived at the bank. Exhausted, they flopped down on the grass.

The group plodded among the wildebeest and zebras' herds across the grassy savanna.

Ceros grazed as he went, but a weak Leo and Pala trailed behind. Each step looked like it caused great effort as they limped towards a waterhole.

While drinking, Leo raised his head and looked at Pala. "By the way, fantastic driving, Pala."

Surprised, Pala looked at Leo. "Really?"

Leo smiled. "Yeah! Where did you learn to drive a car?!"

"Nowhere! It was beginner's luck!" Pala laughed.

Leo laughed, too. "But you did great!"

"You, too," Pala replied.

"By the way, Hmm... I'm... I'm..." Leo took a breath, seemed uneasy, "I'm sorry I was tough on you."

Stunned, Pala smiled. "So, kings can say sorry?"

"Sometimes," Leo sighed with bitterness, "especially when they are dying."

Leo and Pala looked away, taking in their emaciated bodies.

"Or when they lose their kingdom and... their family," Leo added, voice breaking.

"I miss my family, too... But we still have a chance to save our families," Pala expressed.

Leo's eyes shined. He and Pala smiled at each other.

Losalo, Ceros, and Bupha approached them.

"How far is Nairobi?" Bupha asked.

"Can we walk?" Ceros wondered.

"I can't walk anymore. I wish I could fly like Bupha," Losalo panted.

Pala looked around, thinking. Above the trees, she noticed the very top of an air balloon. Her eyes shined. "Fly! I've got an idea!"

24

IN THE SKY

The group lurked behind some trees at the edge of a hot air balloon site. The balloon was still landing on the ground.

A giant balloon hovered above a big, broad basket. Sandbags were attached to the basket, holding it in place.

A short fat pilot talked to a group of tourists.

Pala noticed an older woman holding a pamphlet. On its cover was a photo of Nairobi National Park. "Those are Nairobi photos!" Pala whispered.

"So?" Leo asked.

"It means that these people will go back to Nairobi! So if we can get in this balloon —" Pala replied.

"But how will we get in that thing?" Ceros wondered.

The tourists stood in line to get in the balloon. The Pilot opened the basket door for the passengers.

"We have to go now!" Pala stated.

The animals ran toward the balloon and stood innocently in line. Leo stood just behind the older woman. She turned around and did a double-take when she saw Leo.

"Monster! Monster!" the older woman screamed.

She dropped the pamphlet. It landed on the ground, open to a photo of the Kenyatta International Conference Center. Bupha picked it up with his peck as the tourists started screaming.

"Monsters! Run!" tourists shouted.

Chaos erupted, and the tourists ran in all directions. The pilot tried to run, but Leo shoved him into the balloon. Pala, Ceros, Losalo, and Bupha followed.

The pilot trembled in the corner of the balloon as the animals surrounded him.

Bupha dropped the pamphlet in front of the pilot. Leo pointed at the Kenyatta International Conference Center's photo.

The pilot shook his head. Leo answered him with a SNARL.

The pilot whimpered and nodded emphatically.

****

The balloon flew over Maasai Mara plains.

Leo lay on the floor while the others peered over the side of the basket taking in the spectacular vistas.

Losalo moved to stand on the pilot's shoulder. The

pilot tried to guide the balloon but ventured a glance at Losalo. Then Leo SNARLED, and the pilot looked away.

The mountains merged with the golden plains and the rivers to form an awe-inspiring scene. Ceros, with Bupha on his horns, looked out in awe. Pala appeared beside him.

"I never imagined I'd see the jungle from the sky! Did you, Ceros?" Pala asked.

"Of course not! I never imagined any of this," he smiled gratefully at Pala, "you made me see a new world."

Ceros turned back to the view, but Pala kept looking admirably at him.

She was feeling love for the first time. In her mind, she wondered if Ceros would feel the same since she was so ugly and scary. *And even if he loved me back, she thought. I might die soon.*

At this moment, Ceros stared tenderly at Pala. He was also thinking passionately about her. *Her look might be odd, but she is so brave,* he thought. *She had opened my eyes as no one else had.*

Bupha looked between Pala and Ceros. In his mind, he was unsure if he welcomed the love he saw blossoming between Pala and Ceros or if it should make him jealous. Ceros was his only family, and he didn't want to lose him.

Losalo watched the scenery below, thinking about Vandella and wondering if she still loved him. He thought he knew everything but realized that he only knew a small slice of the world.

Leo was thinking of all the new things that he was feeling: love, fear, gratitude, and respect towards the others. Like his comrades, he was unsure if he liked these changes in him or yearned for the old way of life he had. One thing was for sure: he missed his family desperately.

Even if our heroes' thoughts and feelings were different at that moment, but they were all turning about one thing: LOVE.

25

HILTON NAIROBI

By night, the hot air balloon flew over Nairobi. The Kenyatta International Conference Center and the I&M Bank Tower appeared in the distance.

Leo and Pala had LESS THAN 12 HOURS LEFT BEFORE STARVING. Pala stared admirably at dazzling lights and skyscrapers. "It's Nairobi."

"Are you sure, Pala?" Ceros asked.

"I remember these buildings," Pala replied.

Still stunned, the Pilot opened the parachute valve, and the AIR STREAMED out of the top of the balloon. The balloon began to descend. The Kenyan Parliament buildings, the Holy Family Cathedral, the blue I&M Bank Tower, and the Kenyatta Conference Center all surrounded the crowded City Square. In the middle, the Jomo Kenyatta statue overlooked a big fountain.

A BRIDE and groom took photos in front of the statue. The bride looked up, and her eyes widened.

Other passersby gathered to point as the balloon floated into sight above the buildings, finally landing in the middle of the square.

The basket door flew open, and Leo stepped out first, followed by Pala. The bride gasped at Pala's protruding teeth.

"Monsters! Monsters!" the bride screamed. The groom grabbed his wife, and people running in all directions.

A police car pulled up, and the Police Chief, a tall black man, got out. He pointed to the animals. "There! Get them!"

More cars pulled up, and a dozen policemen spilled out. The animals took off. One policeman took out his handgun.

"No guns! There are too many people around," the Police Chief ordered.

The policemen pulled out their sticks and tasers and gave chase down a crowded two-way street.

Leo, Pala, and their comrades ran on the City-Hall Way. They weaved frenetically between cars and pedestrians. The policemen were still behind them.

People screamed and jumped out of the way; cars crashed as they veered out of the way. The scene was utterly chaotic. Leo led the others in a frantic sprint towards the Hilton Nairobi Hotel. Leo and the others burst into the hotel's reception area. They made for an open elevator as tourists screamed and fled.

Leo jumped in the elevator just as the doors closed, but the others didn't make it in. They looked at one another, terrified, and then dispersed.

Pala and Losalo went left, Ceros and Bupha to the right.

A few moments after, the police entered and looked around.

"Be careful! We don't want anyone to get hurt," the Police Chief ordered his men. He tried to reassure the terrified guests, "Don't be afraid! The situation is under control!"

****

An older white woman was pressed against the side of the elevator, looking at Leo with terror.

He stared at her, and she fainted.

BING as the door opened.

Leo hopped into a corridor, noticing a police officer at its end. The policeman's back was to Leo, allowing him to dodge into an open door at his right.

Leo entered a conference room and froze.

Eight well-dressed people sat around a table as a man stood before a big screen. He projected a photo of a lion.

Leo passed in front of the screen, stopping to stare at the lion photo. He SNARLED at it, and the room erupted in screams.

The policeman heard the SCREAMS and ran to

the conference room.

He entered the now empty room. He slowly passed the screen.

Leo suddenly jumped out at the cop, hitting him with his front paw. The policeman fell to the ground, and Leo bounded out of the room.

****

Pala and Losalo crept into a massage room. It was tranquil. They almost didn't notice that a woman lay face-down on the table, her body wrapped only in a towel. "Mamma mia!" Losalo shouted. His eyeballs popped out.

"Shhhhhh!" Pala hit Losalo with her front leg. He stumbled and fell on the woman's body.

The woman startled and turned over, seeing Losalo. She screamed.

****

Ceros and Bupha entered a restroom. Bupha pointed to a stall.

"Let's hide in this box," Bupha whispered.

Ceros saw the space between the stall door and the floor. "I'll enter from below. You go from above!"

In the stall, a man was sitting on the toilet. He gasped when he saw Ceros' snout poking under the door. He looked up to see Bupha hovering above.

He screamed and burst out of the stall.

Ceros and Bupha watched him go. Bupha sniffed the air and winced. "Ufff! What a smell!"

****

Pala and Losalo almost collided with Leo, Ceros, and Bupha in front of the hotel restaurant. The place was packed. A big open buffet table sat in the corner, and police milled about.

The Police Chief looked up. "There! Catch them!"

The animals jumped in all directions as the police pursued them. They knocked into tables, toppling dishware and food amid the screaming guests.

Pala bounded towards a set of swinging double doors. It was the hotel's kitchen.

Leo, Ceros, Bupha, and Losalo followed Pala. They sprint through kitchen staff, hitting trays and equipment and knocking waiters from their feet.

"The door!" Pala noted.

The animals sprinted towards the back door, leaving chaos in their wake.

26

PALA INJURED

The animals burst out of the Hilton Nairobi's building and onto an empty side street. The policemen appeared, right on their tail. The Police Chief noticed no one was about and waved frantically to his men. "Shoot them!"

The policemen began to SHOOT at the fleeing animals. They ran in zigzags to avoid the bullets.

"The dream!" Pala said to Leo.

"What?!" Leo asked.

The SHOOTING was deafening. Leo noticed what looked like a big box, hanging on the side of a skyscraper about 100 meters away. It was an electric winch.

"Get to the box!" Leo shouted.

Losalo looked back. The policemen were closer.

"I'll try to stall them," Losalo stated.

Leo, Pala, Ceros, and Bupha jumped into the winch. As they entered, Ceros accidentally hit the control switch. The MACHINE HUMMED and began to rise.

"What the hell is this?!" Bupha wondered, stunned.

Three policemen approached at a run. Losalo wrapped a barbel around one policeman's leg.

The man shuddered as Losalo electrocuted him. Losalo flung out his other barbel, zapping another policeman. The last man standing pulled his gun. "Uh, Oh!" Losalo trembled, terrified.

Ceros watched the policeman pull his gun on Losalo. He climbed up on the winch's side.

"Where are you going?" Bupha shouted.

"Losalo's in trouble!" Ceros replied.

Leo and Pala turned just in time to watch Ceros jump. Bupha flew after him.

****

Ceros leaped onto the policeman and jabbed him with his horn. The man dropped his gun with a cry of pain.

Losalo covered his relief with a smug strut. "You know, Ceros! I was just about to electrocute him! Thank you anyway, though."

Losalo and Ceros climbed back up the siding to the winch, now about three meters up.

Ceros made a big jump the rest of the way. Bupha flew up to meet them. Just as they piled back in the winch, BULLETS WHIZZED. Bupha ducked down into the box. "Hahaha! We survived!"

"Youpiiii! I did it! I'm great!" Losalo cheered.

Bupha jabbed at Losalo with his peck.

"Ouch! OK! We did it!" Losalo yelped.

Leo and Ceros laughed.

"What now, Pala?!" Ceros asked Pala.

There was no answer.

"Pala?!"

They turned to see Pala lying amid a pool of blood.

"Oh, my God. You are wounded!" Ceros gasped.

****

The winch arrived at the skyscraper's roof. Ceros helped Pala off the winch with the others. Suddenly, they heard a multitude of ECHOING FOOTSTEPS from the roof stairwell.

Bupha flew to the open door and looked inside. "They're coming!"

"What are we going to do?" Losalo asked Leo.

Leo looked around. He saw a high building under construction beside the skyscraper they stood on. A several meters-wide gap separated the two roofs.

"We jump," Leo stated.

"But... Pala!" Bupha hesitated.

"I'll carry her," Ceros said.

Ceros tried to hold Pala between his teeth but in vain.

"Leave me!" Pala said, delirious.

"I'll carry you!" Leo told Pala.

"But –" Pala replied.

"We came together. We return together," Leo stated.

The policemen's VOICES and FOOTSTEPS grew louder.

"Hurry up!" Losalo shouted.

Losalo took a flying leap, landing unsteadily on the opposite roof. Ceros hesitated.

"Jump. We've no time," Leo kindly reassured Ceros, "don't worry! Everything is going to be OK".

Ceros took a deep breath and jumped. He landed on the other side, meeting Bupha as he flew across.

Leo carried Pala in his mouth as if she was a cub. He looked behind him as police streamed onto the roof from the stairwell door. Guns raised.

Leo, carrying Pala between his teeth, made a significant jump to the other building. A GUNSHOT flew just over his head.

Leo landed hard with Pala on the roof of the building under construction. He staggered, dropping her and falling. Ceros helped him up, pointed to an open door in the corner.

Leo and his comrades descended the stairs. THEY GOT ON LANGATA ROAD.

****

Langata Road was a sparsely crowded two-way

route lined by high trees and bushes. Leo limped down the green traffic island, Pala still in his mouth. Losalo and Ceros followed with Bupha flying over them.

"I think we're lost!" Losalo shouted.

Pala raised her head weakly, seeing a small building with a truss roof. A lion's statue loomed in front of its iron gate beside a sign: "NAIROBI NATIONAL PARK - MAIN GATE ENTRANCE."

Pala pointed painfully to the building, "There!"

The others looked.

"Are you sure, Pala? Ceros asked.

Pala nodded.

They approached the gate, slowing as they noticed guards patrolling in front of it.

"How are we gonna enter without they see us?" Ceros wondered.

"I'll tour around. Look for a way in," Bupha stated.

Bupha flew over the gate. He returned a few moments later and pointed to a low gate, "Here!"

Ceros helped Leo get Pala over the low, unguarded wall. Bupha landed on Ceros' horns.

Leo and his comrades got in NAIROBI NATIONAL PARK.

Leo carried Pala as he staggered down a tree-lined asphalt path with the others. Pala's eyes opened, catching a wooden sign in a truss form: "NAIROBI ANIMAL ORPHANAGE." She pointed, "Dr. Caren treated me here."

Leo carried Pala, trailing behind the others.

They passed rows of cages containing lions, cheetahs, monkeys, and baboons. When the caged animals saw Leo and his friends, they began to SHOUT.

A few GUARDS manning the cages looked up, seeing our animal crew. They drew their guns.

****

Meanwhile, Dr. Caren was in her Lab, staring intently into a microscope.

Her CELLPHONE RINGED, jarring her. She saw the name on the caller ID and picked it up. "Hello, Prof. Williams!"

"Did you get the lakes' water analysis reports?" Dr. Caren heard Prof. Williams's voice demand.

"Unfortunately, the results are all negative. Do you have any news? " Dr. Caren asked.

"No. I'm afraid we're looking for a ghost," Prof. Williams answered.

At this moment, Dr. Caren heard SHOUTS from outside. "Hold on, Dad."

Dr. Caren walked up to the guards, still holding the animals at gunpoint. "What's going on?" she asked the guards.

The guards turned.

"We found these weird animals!" One guard answered.

Dr. Caren moved closer, peering closely at our friends. Leo, carrying Pala, was in the front. Behind him stood Losalo and Ceros. Bupha hid between Ceros' horns.

Dr. Caren's eyes raked over Leo's odd form and Pala's fangs. Pala opened her eyes, seeing Dr. Caren. She smiled weakly.

"Is this she?" Ceros asked Pala.

Leo carefully put Pala on the ground.

Dr. Caren noticed Pala's injury and slowly pulled out her cell. She dialed. "Dad? There's something you should see."

27

THE PUZZLE

It was night. Dr. Caren stood in her lab, hovering over Pala on a medical bed. Leo lay down in a corner. His bones looked even more sharp and visible. Losalo bounded about the room while Ceros very still lay beside Pala. He looked anxiously at her. Bupha sat on his horns.

"Don't worry, my friend! She's going to be OK," Bupha said to Ceros.

Prof. Williams took in the scene from a corner. "Did you do the DNA test?"

"Yes! We've got a female impala, a male lion, and a catfish." Dr. Caren pointed to Pala, Leo, and Losalo, respectively. She tied Pala's wounded leg with a bandage.

"Now, you'll be fine, my baby," Dr. Caren tenderly consoled Pala.

"So, these animals are part of the puzzle we're trying to solve," Prof. Williams supposed.

Dr. Caren nodded. She noticed a seal on Pala's leg written on it: "KWS - Nairobi."

Dr. Caren caressed Pala. "So, we're old friends!"

Losalo leaped on the light switch and plunged the room into darkness. His barbels glowed through the black.

"What's this?!" Prof. Williams wondered, stunned.

Prof. Williams switched the light on and off several times. Losalo's barbels glowed when the room was dark. Prof. Williams and Dr. Caren exchanged a curious look. Prof. Williams opened his bag and retrieved a Geiger Counter. He passed the sensor over Losalo's barbels. "My God! These barbels are radioactive! Caren, could you please get a blood sample from this frog... I mean catfish?"

Dr. Caren prepped a syringe and plunged the needle into Losalo's side. "Ouch! Maledizione!" Losalo screamed.

Dr. Caren walked to a table and put Losalo's sample in a liquid chromatograph. Results flew across the screen. "There's a high concentration of a radioactive chemical in the blood," she wondered, "this is strange! Why didn't we find this chemical in the other animals we checked over the two last days?"

"Maybe somebody directly exposed this catfish to a radioactive chemical. That might explain why the concentration of that material is very high in the catfish's blood," Prof. Williams suggested.

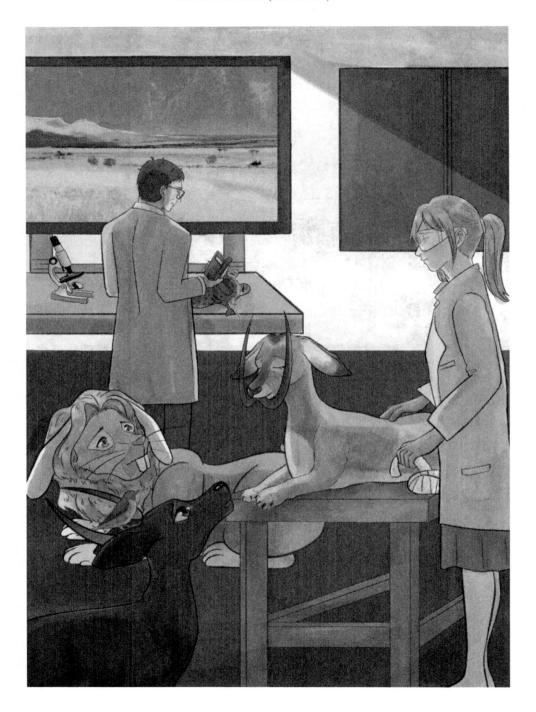

Prof. Willimas was right. REMEMBER?! When the golden rock dropped on Losalo's head, and he smelled it.

Dr. Caren's eyes shined. "We now have a blood sample containing the chemical component we were looking for. I think we may be ready to prepare our vaccine.

"How long does it take?"

"Eight hours, hopefully!"

"Perfect. Meanwhile, I'll work on the chemical we found in this catfish's barbels to prepare the antimatter. Then, we'll put it in the lake, so it stops the chemical's destructive effect," Prof. Williams explained.

Prof. Williams checked his bag. "I think I have most of the instruments required. But maybe I'll need to use your lab, Caren."

Dr. Caren smiled. "You're welcome to it, Prof. Williams."

Dr. Caren turned to examine Losalo's blood sample under a microscope. Prof. Williams put Losalo on another table. He took off one of Losalo's barbels.

Losalo painfully screamed. "Ouch! Nooooo! Not my barbels!"

Prof. Williams freed Losalo, who hurried over to a corner to check his barbels. Nearby, Leo slumped down, breath heavy.

Ceros tenderly nuzzled Pala, but she hardly smiled.

Bupha watched them.

Prof. Williams examined the barbel with some radioactive instruments.

****

EIGHT HOURS LATER, Dr. Caren filled a syringe with the vaccine. "I think we're ready."

Dr. Caren approached Pala and gently injected her. Prof. Williams observed.

The animals stared worriedly at Pala. But nothing happened.

Dr. Caren looked up at her dad, disappointed.

Prof. Williams thought a moment. "Maybe there's another chemical in that compound."

Dr. Caren turned back to the animals. "Let's recheck them."

Dr. Caren manually checked the animals' bodies. Prof. Williams passed his Geiger Counter over them. When he arrived at Pala, the Geiger flashed.

"This impala has radioactive material in her body," Prof. Williams declared.

Dr. Caren checked Pala's body. She found a small golden patch under her front paw. "Look at this, Dad!"

Prof. Williams passed his Geiger Counter over Pala's paw. The Geiger Counter flashed, and Prof. Williams smiled at Dr. Caren.

"I'll take a blood sample," Dr. Caren said.

Dr. Caren extracted some blood and examined it in the chromatograph. Dr. Caren looked at the results, confused. "There's nothing in her blood."

"So, this impala has a chemical trace on her paw, but not in her blood," Prof. Williams supposed.

"What does this mean?"

"It means she didn't swallow the chemical directly. Maybe she just stepped on it," Prof. Williams explained.

REMEMBER?! At the golden lake, when Pala trampled through the magic powder that Pitton had dropped.

Dr. Caren stared at Pala, thinking. "If we find where she trampled on the chemical, maybe we can find traces of it still there. Then we can see the other part of the compound."

"We'll have the vaccine, and the antimatter," Prof. Williams stated.

Dr. Caren's eyes shined. "So, we still have a chance to save these animals and the whole jungle." "But how will we find the source?" she asked.

Prof Williams mulled this over. "Let's suppose that someone directly exposed this catfish to the first chemical. And the impala tramples on the other. So, we can assume the chemical compound was thrown at the same place."

"You mean the impala drank from the lake where this catfish lived?" Dr. Caren asked.

"Maybe, or nearby a body of water," Prof.

Williams suggested.

Prof. Williams opened his bag and removed a tablet. "Caren, bring me the catfish's DNA!"

Dr. Caren brought him a pipette tip. Prof. Williams showed his tablet to Dr. Caren.

"This is DNA GPS. We'll put the catfish's DNA sample in this slot. So, the screen will show us the catfish's homeland," Prof. Williams explained.

Prof. Williams emptied Losalo's DNA sample in the tablet's side slot. A photo of the Golden Lake with its coordinates appeared on the screen.

"This could be our source. It's three hundred and fifty kilometers from here," Prof. Williams suggested.

"Three hundred fifty?! These animals will die in two hours. We'd need a helicopter or something —" Dr. Caren said, worried.

"Don't worry! I'll handle it."

Prof. Williams pulled out his phone and dialed. He smiled at Dr. Caren as he murmured into the phone. He handed up. "The helicopter will be ready in ten minutes."

Dr. Caren looked worried. She turned to stare at the animals, who all now slept soundly. Their SNORES filled the air.

28

A FACE-OFF WITH PITTON

In the morning, the loud WHIRL of a HELICOPTER was heard as it slowly descended to land beside the Golden Lake.

Prof. Williams and Dr. Caren hopped out of the copter, leading the animals. Leo and Pala could barely walk. Their spines and hip bones looked like they might poke out of their skin.

Leo and Pala had LESS THAN 30 MINUTES LEFT BEFORE STARVING.

Ceros stared sadly at the limping Pala. Bupha was on his back.

A dejected Losalo jumped next to Ceros.

"Oh, Mio Dio! How will I face my people with this missed barbel?!" Losalo blubbered.

Bupha glared at Losalo.

Prof. Williams began to scan the place with his Geiger Counter. It flashed as it hit a spot on the lake's bank. Prof. Williams saw a light powder in the grass. "I found it!" he shouted.

He scraped the chemical powder into some glassware.

"I'll mix that with the catfish's blood. I think we can now prepare our vaccine," Dr. Caren declared.

"And I'll prepare the antimatter," Prof. Williams stated.

Dr. Caren opened her bag, removing the pipette tip containing Losalo's blood.

She shook some of the powder into the pipette tip. She put it in a scientific-looking instrument.

Meanwhile, Prof. Williams hurried to prepare the antimatter nearby. After a while, Prof. Williams raised his glassware. "It's done," he said gleefully.

Pala suddenly stumbled and then collapsed.

"Pala! Pala!" Ceros gasped.

Leo let out a moan, and he too fell to the ground. Dr. Caren rushed over, looking up at her dad in a panic.

"They're dying," Dr. Caren shouted.

"Have you prepared the vaccine?" Prof. Williams asked, worried.

"Almost!"

Dr. Caren hurried back to her task.

Ceros shook Pala. "No, Pala! Please don't die!"

Losalo and Bupha watched on, frozen and tearful.

After a few tense minutes, Dr. Caren hurried forward with a needle. She injected Pala with it. Then Leo.

She stepped back, and she and Prof. Williams

watched on. Nothing happened.

"What's wrong?" Prof. Williams wondered.

"I don't know!" Dr. Caren replied, confused.

"Let's see what happens when we put the antimatter in the water," Prof. Williams stated.

He grabbed the glassware and approached the lake.

At this moment, they heard Pitton's voice from behind.

"You don't have time!" Pitton said.

Prof. Williams and Dr. Caren turned and saw Pitton step out of the treeline with Sett at his side.

"It's been a while, Professor Williams," Pitton replied.

"Pitton? I knew this was you," Prof. Williams stated, teeth gritted.

"I never doubted your intelligence," Pitton chuckled.

"Listen, Pitton. We've got to stop this. You're destroying the jungle, and the animals —" Prof. Williams said.

"Who cares about animals? I only care about *this*," Pitton interrupted.

He showed a gold bar to Prof. Williams.

The professor's eyes widened. "Pitton, please. You're destroying a whole life for... gold?"

Pitton shrugged and approached Prof. Williams. "Give me the antimatter."

"Never!"

Pitton smiled coldly. "So, you've left me no choice," he pointed to Sett, "kill them!"

****

Sett SNARLED wildly. He stalked towards Prof. Williams and Dr. Caren.

Leo and Pala lay motionless and unnoticed behind Pitton and Sett. Losalo jumped between some bushes.

But Ceros didn't move. He stayed beside Pala. Trembling, Bupha hid between Ceros' horns.

Dr. Caren grabbed her father's hand. Her eyes filled with terrified tears as Sett slunk closer. But suddenly, blinded them all.

Sett and Pitton turned to see Leo transforming in a flash of light. His teeth grew, his ears shrunk, and his hind legs returned to normal.

When he opened his eyes... he was a lion. He ROARED.

Dr. Caren and prof. Williams exchanged amazed looks.

Losalo cheered and clapped his fins. "Yahoooo! Our king is back!"

Sett whimpered as Leo advanced.

"Well, well, well, Sett! It has been a long time since we met! Maybe two days?" Leo said.

Sett's jaw dropped.

"Won't you welcome me back, my friend?" Leo mocked, "never mind! I'll do it my way."

Leo hit Sett with his paw, flipping him over on his back. Terrified, Sett scrambled to his feet and took off, leaving Pitton alone.

Leo slowly turned to appraise Pitton.

"Do you still want the antimatter?!" Prof. Williams sarcastically asked Pitton.

Pitton glared at Prof. Williams and Dr. Caren. "We're not done yet!"

Pitton ran. SOBS filled the air. Everyone turned to see Ceros crying over a still Pala. Prof. Williams gripped his daughter's hand.

"I think she's dead," Prof. Williams said.

Suddenly, shining rays spread across Pala's body. Her tusks retracted, and her hooves returned to normal. When she opened her eyes, the first thing she saw was Ceros looking at her.

"I didn't realize you are so beautiful, Pala," Ceros said lovingly.

Pala smiled timidly. "I'm back," she whispered.

Ceros bumped his head, affectionately against hers. Prof. Williams and Dr. Caren watched gleefully.

"You did it, Caren," Prof. Williams cheered.

Caren smiled.

"Now..." Prof. Williams approached the Golden Lake and emptied the antimatter onto its surface.

The WATER BUBBLED. Shining rays slowly spread across the lake. Dr. Caren, Prof. Williams, and the animals watched with astonishment.

It all simmered for a moment and then went returns to normal. Leo turned to the others with a smile.

"Now, let's find our families!" Leo said.

Leo, Losalo, Ceros, and Bupha bounded away, but Pala stayed. She and Dr. Caren shared a tender look.

Dr. Caren slowly reached a hand out and caressed her snout. Pala licked her hand, then leaned forward and licked her face.

Dr. Caren laughed.

"Come on, Pala!" Leo shouted.

Pala leaped away. Dr. Caren and Prof. Williams stood alone on the lake's shore.

Prof. Williams tenderly put a hand on Dr. Caren's shoulder. "Let's take a tour in the jungle and see how animals are reacting to our treatment."

29

ORDER'S BACK

A few days later, a new sunny day was rising on Mount Kenya. Mixed herds of zebras, wildebeests, and impalas were grazing in the Laikipia Plateau.

Dr. Caren walked beside Prof. Williams, who read the news on an iPad.

The screen showed the headline: "A group of weird animals prevents a terrorist attempt on Maasai Mara."

A photo, clearly shot on a cell phone, accompanied it of Pala during the car chase. She was behind the wheel of the Jeep, with the other animals comically terrified behind her.

Prof. Williams smiled. "Your friends are famous."

Dr. Caren looked at the iPad and grinned. "They saved the jungle. Even if they didn't know they were doing it."

"Do you think they've gone back to normal?" Prof. Williams wondered.

At the Golden Lake, underwater, Losalo, back in his catfish form, hovered in the middle of a catfish circle. Vandella was beside him.

"Afterward! One hundred men with guns were chasing us. All my friends were scared. But I beat them alone," Losalo boasted.

"Wow! One hundred?!" the catfish shouted.

"I think they were two hundred!" Losalo swaggered.

Vandella proudly applauded her husband with her fins. "Tell them how you jumped twenty meters in the air."

"Twenty-*two* meters," Losalo interrupted, angry. "Oh, Mamma mia! It was a significant jump, and..." he bragged. Losalo closed his eyes and added theatrically, "Because of this jump, I missed one of my barbels."

"Ohhhh!" the catfish gasped.

"I know it's a great sacrifice on my part. But I'm proud my barbel saved the jungle," Losalo said in a fake humbleness.

****

Far away, the hot sun beat down on the Savanna. Pala and Aipa leaped across the plain together. They stopped laughing. "Pala! You saved the jungle. You acted like a heroine. I'm so proud of you," Aipa congratulated her daughter.

Pala smiled. She bumped her head, affectionately against her mother's. She looked up as Ceros and Bupha approached.

"I think it's time to say goodbye," Ceros said.

"What? Why?!" Pala asked, shocked.

"You've got your form back; you're with your family. And I'm... a stranger."

"You're not anymore," Aipa replied.

Ceros looked surprised.

"You saved my daughter's life. You're part of the family."

Pala warmly nuzzled her mom. Ceros looked at Bupha, concerned.

"Bupha was with me! I can't stay without him!" Ceros stated.

Bupha landed on Aipa's head to peck tenderly at her eyes.

"It's OK! You can stay too," Aipa laughed.

She bounced off, leaving Pala and Ceros alone. They both exchanged bashful looks. Pala was about to speak when Mela leaped between them.

"Someone's happy here! Pala, do you love this handsome guy?" Mela asked with a sly smile.

Pala looked embarrassed. "Mela, shut up!" she turned to Ceros, "Ceros, let me introduce you to Mela, the silliest impala in the jungle."

They all laughed. Suddenly, Mela's smile slid from her face and her eyes filled with horror. Pala turned and saw Leo, Venata, and Catu approaching.

"Hi!" Pala said. She reassured Mela, "Don't worry. Leo's a friend."

Mela swallowed.

"Hello, Ceros. How are you doing?" Leo asked.

"Great, my lord!"

Leo looked sincerely at Pala. "I wanted to thank you for everything. You saved my life. You helped me restore my kingdom and my family."

"Me?"

"You."

Pala flushed and looked down. "You're the brave one. You acted like a real king."

"We both did. Together," Leo replied.

They stared at one another. Pala playfully nudged him.

"You're the king. I'm just an impala."

"We all have a power inside us. We just need to discover it. And I think you have," Leo said.

Pala smiled broadly, her eyes shining. "So, we can stay friends?"

Leo nodded. He knocked his head softly against Pala's. She nodded to Ceros and Mela, and the three bounded off.

Catu watched them uncertainly. "How can a lion and impala be friends? You told me that we rule with fear."

"I was wrong, son," Leo replied.

He turned to fix Venata with a loving gaze. "We rule with love."

Venata smiled.

Catu jumped between his parents. "So, fathers say the wrong thing?"

"They often do!" Leo whispered conspiratorially.

They all laughed.

But they didn't know that someone was watching them.

On a woodland hill, near the savanna, two human eyes peered through the shrubs.

A face slowly emerged.

It was Pitton. He smiled coldly.

To be continued

CRAZY JUNGLE (Leo & Pala)

ABOUT THE AUTHOR

Dr. Haytham Ragab is an author, an animation screenwriter, a journalist, and an academic researcher. He obtained his master's and doctorate from Canadian universities. He worked for prestigious media and high-caliber academic institutions in Canada, France, and Egypt. He has always been concerned with social justice, gender equity, power, and empowerment ideas, which appear in his intellectual production. The conflict between love and fear, integration and discrimination, selfishness and collaboration are the main themes elaborated in his writings. As Dr. Haytham is Egyptian-Canadian, this multiculturalism makes him concerned by the civilizations dialogue issue as he believes that the world is so wide to include all of us together. Dr. Haytham is married and has two daughters.

Printed in Great Britain
by Amazon

76918829R00078

The Split History of

QUEEN ELIZABETH I

AND

MARY, QUEEN OF SCOTS

QUEEN ELIZABETH I's PERSPECTIVE

BY NICK HUNTER

CONTENT CONSULTANT:
Dr William Hepburn
Teaching Assistant at the University of the Highlands and Islands
and Graduate Teaching Assistant at the University of Glasgow

Raintree is an imprint of Capstone Global Library Limited, a company incorporated in England and
Wales having its registered office at 264 Banbury Road, Oxford, OX2 7DY – Registered company
number: 6695582

www.raintree.co.uk
myorders@raintree.co.uk

Text © Capstone Global Library Limited 2017
The moral rights of the proprietor have been asserted.

Edited by Helen Cox Cannons
Designed by Philippa Jenkins
Original illustrations © Capstone Global Library Ltd 2016
Picture research by Kelly Garvin
Production by Victoria Fitzgerald
Originated by Capstone Global Library Ltd
Printed and bound in China

ISBN 978 1 4747 2670 2 (hardback)
20 19 18 17 16
10 9 8 7 6 5 4 3 2 1

ISBN 978 1 4747 2674 0 (paperback)
21 20 19 18 17
10 9 8 7 6 5 4 3 2 1

ACKNOWLEDGEMENTS

We would like to thank the following for permission to reproduce photographs:
Elizabeth I's Perspective: Alamy: GL Archive, 27, Heritage Image Partnership Ltd, 13, Historical Images
Archive, 7, Mary Evans Picture Library, 5, The National Trust Photolibrary, 19; Bridgeman Images/The
Pope's Bull against the Queen in 1570, Hulsen, Fresrich van (c.1580-1660)/Private Collection, 20; Getty
Images/Hulton Archive, 24; Newscom: Agence Quebec Presse, 8, 17, Glasshouse Images, 11, Ken Welsh,
25, World History Archive, 15, 23, 29; Superstock: Superstock, cover (bottom), World History Archive,
cover (top); The Image Works/Pictures From History, 21.
Mary, Queen of Scots' Perspective: Alamy/GL Archive, 17, julie woodhouse, 23, The National Trust
Photolibrary, 24; Bridgeman Images: Henry Stuart, Lord Darnley, Second husband of Mary Queen of
Scots, Linton, Sir James Dromgole/Private Collection/Look and Learn, 13, Map of Edinburgh from
Civitates Orbis Terrarum by George Braun and Franz Hogenberg/DeAgostini Picture Library, 15,
Miniature of Mary Queen of Scots, c1560, Clouet, Francois/Victoria & Albert Museum, London, UK, 9;
Getty Images: Culture Club, 19, Hulton Archive, 29, The Print Collector, 20; North Wind Picture Archive,
11; Shutterstock: Georgios Kollidas, 5, Heartland Arts, 6; Superstock: Superstock, cover (top), World
History Archive, cover (bottom...

We would like to thank Dr Wi[...]   s book.

Every effort has been made to c[...]   Any omissions
will be rectified in subsequent p[...]

All the internet addresses (URL[...]   However,
due to the dynamic nature of th[...]   ve changed or
ceased to exist since publication[...]   is may cause
readers, no responsibility for an[...]   ublisher.

Contents

SHARED RESOURCES

CHAPTER 1

DANGEROUS NEIGHBOURS

In May 1568, Queen Elizabeth had a decision to make. Her cousin Mary Stuart was no longer Queen of Scotland. Powerful Scottish nobles had forced her from power. Mary had secretly fled to northern England. Should Elizabeth help Mary?

Elizabeth sympathized with her cousin. If the Scots could depose their queen, Elizabeth's English subjects might have the same idea. But there was much more at stake. Mary's arrival in England raised questions about religious battles and the troubled history between England and Scotland. If she got it wrong, Elizabeth's life could be under threat.

CENTURIES OF DISCONTENT

England's kings and queens had faced centuries of discontent from the upstart Scots. This included raids and attacks on northern England, and support for rebels against the English monarch. It was not just the Scots that worried Elizabeth and her advisers. Scotland was an ally of an even greater enemy – France.

There were two ways of solving this problem. Elizabeth's grandfather King Henry VII chose the peaceful way. He arranged for his eldest daughter, Margaret, to marry King James IV of Scotland. This marriage would unite the English Tudor family and the Scottish Stuarts. That was the idea anyway.

KINGDOMS AT WAR

In 1513, Margaret Tudor's brother King Henry VIII tried the other approach to the problem – war. He took on both parts of the "Auld Alliance", France and Scotland, at the same time. Scotland's King James IV was killed in the English victory at the Battle of Flodden. In 1542, Henry launched another attack on Scotland after Scotland's King James V had refused Henry's invitation to meet him. James V was defeated at the Battle of Solway Moss and died soon afterwards.

Henry VIII and his three children. Edward VI ruled from 1547 until 1553, and was followed by his half-sisters, Queens Mary I and Elizabeth I. Edward was the youngest of the three.

Religion was at the heart of Henry VIII's problems with Scotland. Henry had quarrelled with the Pope. The leader of the Roman Catholic Church would not allow him to divorce his first wife. Henry was determined to get his way and made himself head of a new Protestant Church of England. This made him an enemy to many of Europe's rulers, who were Roman Catholics. They included the new Queen of Scotland, although James V's daughter Mary, Queen of Scots was just a baby.

Henry's latest plan for peace with Scotland was to agree to a marriage between his own baby son, Edward, and Mary, Queen of Scots. But Mary's French mother rejected this solution – Mary could not possibly marry the son of a heretic who had defied the Catholic Church. Henry lost his temper and launched several raids against southern Scotland. When he died in 1547, the problem of Scotland was left for his children to deal with.

AFTER HENRY VIII

King Henry's death did not end the struggle for Scotland. The new King Edward VI was just a boy. His ministers knew that France was keen to control Scotland and surround the English. In September 1547, the English defeated a Scottish army at the Battle of Pinkie, near Edinburgh, Scotland.

This was exactly what the French wanted. They offered money and soldiers to protect Scotland. In return, the young queen would be brought up at the French royal court and marry into the French royal family. This would give the French control of Scotland, and England would be next.

In 1553, Henry VIII's eldest daughter, Mary Tudor, became queen. Mary was a devout Catholic. She was also married to King Phillip II of Spain. As England became Catholic again, the tension between England and Scotland eased. But that all changed when Mary died and her half-sister Elizabeth was crowned in 1558.

The Battle of Pinkie, 1547, was the last major battle between the two kingdoms of England and Scotland.

THE UNLIKELY QUEEN

Elizabeth was not expected to become Queen of England. She was the daughter of King Henry VIII and his second wife, Anne Boleyn. Her mother was executed when Elizabeth was just two years old. After her mother's fall from grace, Elizabeth was third in line to the throne behind her half-brother, Edward VI (reigned 1547-1553), and half-sister, Mary I (reigned 1553-1558).

Elizabeth I as a young woman

CHAPTER 2
THE TWO QUEENS

When Queen Elizabeth I took the throne in 1558, many thought she could not possibly be queen for long. England had no money after a disastrous war with France and its people were affected by bad harvests and outbreaks of plague.

Elizabeth was also a woman. In the 1500s, men usually held power. People believed a queen needed a powerful husband to rule effectively. Elizabeth showed no sign of wanting to get married, and without marriage she would not have children to take over the throne when she died.

RELIGIOUS DIVISIONS

The biggest threat to Elizabeth came from battles over religion. Queen Mary I had made England Catholic again. Not only that, she had hundreds of Protestants executed or burned at the stake. Most Catholics believed that Elizabeth should not be queen at all. They didn't believe her parents had been legally married, and they despised Elizabeth's mother, Anne Boleyn. Catholics were even angrier when Elizabeth passed laws to make the Protestant Church of England the country's official religion.

Many powerful people wanted to get rid of Elizabeth, but they would have to replace her with someone. There were no other living children or grandchildren of Henry VIII. However, there were other descendants of Elizabeth's grandfather Henry VII. One of them was Mary, Queen of Scots. If Elizabeth died, Mary would be next in line to the throne of England.

RIGHTFUL QUEEN OF ENGLAND

Elizabeth's advisers were keen to name Mary as heir to the throne if Elizabeth did not have any children. They feared a civil war if there was no chosen heir, but there were problems to resolve first. For a start, Mary was Queen of Scotland and a Catholic. Worse than that, in 1558 Mary married the son of the King of France. Shortly afterwards, Mary's husband became King Francis II. Francis was not content just to rule France and Scotland. He believed that Mary was also the rightful Queen of England.

When religious turmoil hit Scotland in 1559, English troops were actually welcomed as they arrived to support the Protestant rebels. In July 1560, the two sides agreed to the Treaty of Edinburgh requiring French forces to leave Scotland. France also agreed that Elizabeth was the rightful ruler of England.

Francis II died in 1560 but Elizabeth was not likely to forget his threat to her throne. In 1561, Mary, Queen of Scots left France to return to her kingdom. Elizabeth refused to allow the widowed Mary to travel across England on her way to Scotland. The teenage Queen of Scotland was forced to take a long and dangerous sea journey to Edinburgh.

Mary and Francis II were a huge threat to England's security.

Elizabeth knew that if Mary set foot in England, her Catholic supporters might use this as an excuse to plot against Elizabeth. What's more, Mary had refused to agree to the Treaty of Edinburgh, and so confirm that Elizabeth was rightful Queen of England.

FRIENDS OR RIVALS?

The two queens never met, but they exchanged many letters. Elizabeth asked for a portrait of her cousin. She told a Scottish noble in 1562: "My sister [meaning Mary, Queen of Scots] has no greater desire to see me, than I have to see her. ...I hear of many that we [Elizabeth and Mary] do somewhat resemble [each other], but I take it to be spoken to me for flattery."

William Cecil, Elizabeth's chief minister, thought a meeting would be a bad idea. He worried that personal feelings might get in the way of politics.

MARRIAGE AND MONARCHY

In 1562, Elizabeth caught smallpox, a deadly disease at the time. Her advisers were already worried that the childless queen had no obvious heir. What would happen if she died of smallpox? Mary could be next in line to the throne.

While her advisers tried to persuade their queen to marry, they were also worried about Mary's marriage plans. In 1564, the English representative in Scotland presented an idea to Mary. She could marry Robert Dudley, Earl of Leicester. Dudley had been a close friend of Queen Elizabeth. A marriage between Mary and Dudley could end the troubles between England and Scotland. But Mary ignored Elizabeth's suggestion.

In 1565 she married Henry, Lord Darnley, who was also related to the English royal family. Elizabeth had already decided that if Mary was not going to take up the generous offer to marry Robert Dudley, she would never make Mary her heir. England and Scotland were almost back where they started – argumentative rivals rather than allies.

Robert Dudley had been close friends with Elizabeth I.

CHAPTER 3

COUSIN IN CRISIS

While Queen Elizabeth struggled against any attempts to find Mary a husband, Mary's choice of men proved disastrous. Lord Darnley was famously good looking but he was unreliable, and he soon caused problems for his wife.

Elizabeth was angry that Mary had chosen her own husband. If Mary had followed Elizabeth's advice, relations between England and Scotland would be much better. Darnley's family connections made Mary's claim to be the next Queen of England even stronger.

Scotland's Protestant nobles were also unhappy. They believed that Mary was about to make Scotland Catholic again. Elizabeth may have supported the nobles' plan to stop Scotland becoming a Catholic country again, but she could never support a rebellion against a fellow monarch. If Mary could be toppled, Elizabeth might be next.

William Cecil, Elizabeth's chief minister, may have tried to bring England and Scotland closer together but he did not want Mary to be the next Queen of England.

MURDER IN EDINBURGH

Events at the Scottish court went from bad to worse. Mary's marriage to Darnley started to fall apart, although their son, James, was born on 19 June 1566. Darnley was then involved in a plot that ended with the murder of Mary's secretary, David Riccio. When Darnley was murdered in a huge explosion at Kirk o' Field just outside Edinburgh, Mary's reign was in crisis.

Elizabeth was horrified by what was going on in Scotland. Reports suggested that Mary might have been involved in Darnley's murder. It was well known that Mary hated her husband after Riccio's murder. The Queen of England wrote urgently to her cousin: "I should not do the office of a faithful cousin and friend if I did not urge you to preserve your honour, rather than look through your fingers at revenge on those who have done you that pleasure…"

Elizabeth was saying to her cousin that everyone knew what Mary thought of Darnley. If she failed to punish his murderers, the Scottish people would assume she had been involved. Elizabeth's life and reign had taught her plenty about royal plots and how to stay in power. But Mary didn't listen to Elizabeth's advice. No one knows if Mary knew about Darnley's murder in advance. It certainly looked as if she did when she married the Earl of Bothwell, who was accused of Darnley's murder.

The Scottish people turned on their queen. Mary and Bothwell's army was defeated and Mary was held prisoner at Lochleven Castle and forced to abdicate. Her baby son, James, became king, guided by his uncle the Earl of Moray until he was old enough to rule. Mary escaped captivity but was defeated again in battle. She had almost nowhere left to turn.

ELIZABETH'S DILEMMA

England's queen didn't agree with what her cousin had done but monarchs needed to stick together. Elizabeth believed that kings and queens were chosen by God. She planned to do everything she could to save Mary's throne. She sent her ambassador Nicholas Throckmorton to Scotland to try and argue Mary's case. Elizabeth threatened to seek revenge on Mary's behalf if the Scots did not reinstate her. But there was no way back for Mary.

Elizabeth's attempts to regain Mary's throne for her may have convinced Mary that she would find shelter in England. Besides, it was her only option. She fled Scotland in a boat, disguised as an ordinary working woman, and landed at Workington in Cumbria.

MARY'S JEWELS

Queen Elizabeth was furious when Mary was forced to abdicate, but she also realized that the turmoil weakened Scotland. In 1568, she bought some of Mary's jewels from the Earl of Moray, wearing them in many royal portraits. This showed that she believed Scotland was under England's control.

The elaborate dresses and jewellery worn by Elizabeth in portraits were designed to show her power and wealth.

AN UNWELCOME GUEST

The English were taken by surprise by Mary's arrival. Arguments raged at court about what to do. Elizabeth argued that, even if Mary was her enemy, she could not send her back to certain death in Scotland. She also did not want to risk going to war with the Scots to help Mary regain the crown. Elizabeth was also well aware of the dangers of having a Catholic rival living in her country.

The queen decided that Mary should be her guest. This didn't mean the two would meet – after all, Mary was suspected of murdering her own husband. Instead, she would live somewhere comfortable, far from Elizabeth's court. Mary would not be allowed to travel where she wanted. In effect, she was Elizabeth's prisoner.

In October 1568, Elizabeth set up a commission in York to decide if Mary had been involved in Darnley's murder. The evidence against Mary included a collection of letters that she had supposedly written urging Bothwell to murder her husband. Many people who saw the letters at the time, including Queen Elizabeth herself, were convinced that Mary had written them.

Mary said that an English court could not judge a Queen of Scotland and refused to say anything to defend herself. But the evidence against her was so strong that she could never return to Scotland. Instead, Elizabeth and her ministers ensured that Mary was moved from one country house to another. Elizabeth's advisers warned her that if Mary stayed in one area of the country for too long, she could be a focus for discontented Catholics.

PLOTS AGAINST ELIZABETH

English fears that Mary and her supporters would plot against the queen were often proved to be true. Mary continued to follow the Catholic religion and had contact with the Catholic King Phillip II of Spain, the sworn enemy of England. Elizabeth and her government, on the other hand, had banned Catholicism in England.

Catholic priests were forced to hide in secret rooms and tunnels, such as this one at Baddesley Clinton, Warwickshire.

English plotters involved Mary in their own schemes. There was a plan for Mary to marry Thomas Howard, Duke of Norfolk, one of the most powerful men in the country. The Duke of Norfolk and other nobles were jealous of Elizabeth's chief minister, William Cecil. Many were also secret Catholics. With Norfolk and Mary as leaders, they hoped to challenge Cecil's domination. In October 1569, Norfolk was imprisoned in the Tower of London for his part in the plot.

The plot did not end with Norfolk's arrest. The powerful northern earls launched a full-scale rebellion against Elizabeth in November 1569. Their plan was to replace the queen with Mary. The rebellion almost worked, too. Just in time, Elizabeth sent an army to crush the rebels. They moved Mary away from the scene of the uprising. Elizabeth's revenge was quick and brutal; she had 450 rebels executed and beheaded rebel leader the Earl of Northumberland.

In 1572, the Pope excommunicated Elizabeth. Catholics believed this to be permission from the Pope to rebel against Elizabeth.

Plots also came from abroad. In 1571, a devious scheme was discovered, led by Italian banker Roberto Ridolphi. The plan was to free Mary and make her queen, supported by an uprising in the north and a Spanish invading force. The Duke of Norfolk was involved again, and was this time executed, but Elizabeth gave her cousin one more chance.

SIR FRANCIS WALSINGHAM

Sir Francis Walsingham was Elizabeth's spymaster. His job was to discover and stop plots against the queen. Walsingham set up a network of spies across Europe, particularly in the countries that were England's Catholic enemies. At the time, plotters communicated in person or by using coded letters, which Walsingham's spies would intercept.

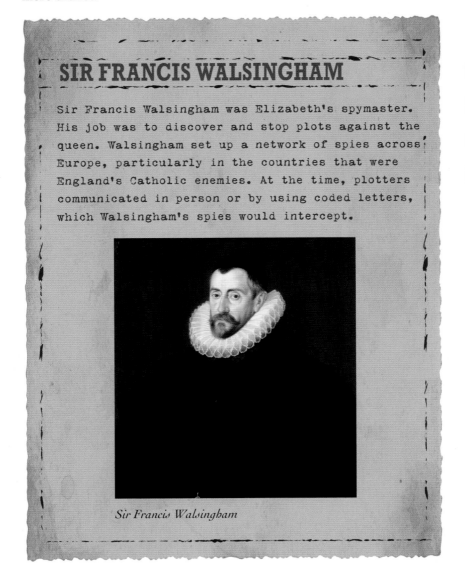

Sir Francis Walsingham

THE BABINGTON PLOT

CHAPTER 5

Elizabeth's ministers, such as Cecil and Walsingham, could see that the plots against Elizabeth would not stop as long as Mary was alive. Religion was at the root of all of them. It was also clear by the 1580s that Elizabeth would never have a child to rule after her.

EUROPE DIVIDED

During the 1570s, religious wars raged across Europe. Protestants fought Catholics in the Netherlands and France. In England, life was made more difficult for those who still followed the Catholic religion. The government feared that the country could be invaded by Spain. If that invasion were successful, Mary would be queen.

Francis Walsingham knew how important Mary was to the Catholic cause and he wanted her out of the way. Walsingham's spies watched the prisoner closely, hoping that she would prove herself to be a traitor.

A NEW REGIME

In 1585, Walsingham decided that Mary's life in captivity had been far too easy. He ordered that she be moved to Chartley House near Sheffield. This new prison would enable Walsingham to monitor Mary's contact with the outside world even more closely.

Walsingham devised a communication route so that Mary could send what she thought were secret letters. The catch was that Walsingham's spies were reading all of Mary's letters.

What they discovered were letters to a London businessman called Anthony Babington. In June 1585, Babington wrote to Mary with details of the latest plot to free her and depose Queen Elizabeth: "Myself with ten gentlemen and a hundred of our followers will undertake the delivery of your royal person from the hands of your enemies."

Mary wrote and received letters from Spain at a time when the Spanish were planning to invade England.

THE FATAL LETTER

Babington was not a successful plotter. All Walsingham had to do was to prove that Mary was involved. When she sent a letter to Babington asking for more details, Walsingham's spies forged an extra section in Mary's handwriting, in which Mary appeared to ask the names of the plotters. When Babington replied and Mary sent an encouraging note, Walsingham had all the proof he needed.

Babington and his fellow plotters were captured and gruesomely executed in public, to warn people from plotting against Elizabeth. Executing common plotters was normal, but ordering the death of a queen chosen by God was something else. What would Elizabeth do with the rebellious Mary?

Many people knew of Babington's plans to overthrow Elizabeth I.

CHAPTER 6

FINAL ACT

he Babington Plot was the last straw for Elizabeth. The queen's enemies were closing in on all sides. Walsingham's decoding of Mary's letters had given Elizabeth the evidence she needed to solve the problem of the Queen of Scots forever.

The English authorities moved Mary to Fotheringhay Castle in Northamptonshire to face trial. There was not much doubt that Mary had plotted with Babington and others, even if Walsingham's forger had invented one of the key pieces of evidence. A few days later, the former Queen of Scotland was found guilty. She would be sentenced to death.

ELIZABETH'S DILEMMA

Londoners celebrated when they heard the news. Parliament and Elizabeth's advisers wanted to execute Mary as soon as possible. Queen Elizabeth had very mixed feelings, though. The queen knew that Mary had plotted against her for years. If she allowed Mary to live she would remain a danger to Elizabeth and England itself, but there were three reasons that stopped her ordering Mary's execution.

First, although they had never met, Mary was family. Elizabeth's own mother, Anne Boleyn, had been executed when she was a baby and this may have affected how she felt. Second, Mary was a queen, chosen by God, as Elizabeth believed. By taking her life, Elizabeth feared she might be breaking God's law. Third, Elizabeth was worried about revenge, either from Mary's supporters at home or overseas.

Elizabeth often hesitated and changed her mind when she had difficult decisions to make. This was one of the biggest decisions of her life and she couldn't bring herself to sign Mary's death warrant for three months. She looked desperately for other solutions to the problem.

William Cecil and Elizabeth's ministers tried hard to convince her that there was no alternative. Meanwhile, ambassadors from France and Scotland, which were now England's friends, urged Elizabeth to show mercy.

Elizabeth finally relented, and on 1 February 1587 she signed Mary's death warrant.

LAST LETTERS

In October 1586, Elizabeth wrote to her cousin Mary. The letter makes it clear that she was angry and felt betrayed by Mary's plotting against her:

"You have in various ways and manners attempted to take my life and bring my kingdom to destruction by bloodshed. I have never proceeded so harshly against you, but have, on the contrary, protected and maintained you like myself."

Elizabeth was probably fooling herself when she wrote that she had "protected and maintained" Mary.

By 1587, Elizabeth was an experienced monarch. She had survived many plots against her.

ELIZABETH'S RAGE

Mary was beheaded at Fotheringhay Castle on 8 February 1587. When Elizabeth was told the news, she flew into a violent rage, blaming everyone around her for killing Mary against her orders. Her ministers hid from her anger. Even William Cecil, her most trusted minister, was not allowed into her presence for six months. Part of Elizabeth's anger was due to remorse about what she had done. However, she was also worried about the future.

FACING THE FUTURE

In the early years of her reign, Elizabeth had allowed Catholics to worship in secret. This had not stopped the plots against her, so severe punishments were introduced for anyone suspected of being a Catholic.

In Spain, King Phillip II had already begun to prepare a fleet of ships to invade England. This invasion plan was about protecting Spain's interests as well as the battle between Catholics and Protestants. Mary's execution strengthened King Phillip's resolve to deal with the heretic Elizabeth. But Phillip's attack against England did not succeed – the Spanish Armada was defeated in 1588.

Mary's execution did not end attacks on Elizabeth from home either. Elizabeth's main weakness was still that there was no clear heir to the throne. By 1587, the queen was getting old by Tudor standards. The question of who would take over from her was becoming more urgent.

When Elizabeth's long reign came to an end with her death on 24 March 1603, the next monarch was King James VI of Scotland, who had taken over the throne as a baby from his mother, Mary. He now became King James I of England.

Mary lost the battle with Elizabeth, but the first King of England and Scotland in 1603 was not a Tudor, but Mary, Queen of Scots's son, James.

INDEX

GLOSSARY

ABDICATE—resign from position as king or queen

ARISTOCRAT—member of upper class of rich and powerful families in a society

ASSASSINATE—murder an important person for political or religious reasons

BARON—lowest-ranked noble

CATHOLIC—Christian who is a member of the Roman Catholic Church, led by the Pope

CIPHER—method of creating coded or secret documents or letters

COURTIER—member of the court of a monarch

EXCOMMUNICATE—officially exclude a person from the Catholic Church (by the Pope)

HEIR—someone who will take over the responsibilities or titles of another person on their death, such as an heir to the throne who will take over as monarch from a previous king or queen

HERETIC—person with religious beliefs that go against the teachings of the main Church

INTERCEPT—prevent something from reaching its destination

MARTYR—someone who is persecuted or dies because of his or her religious beliefs

MONARCH—king or queen

NOBLE—member of the leading or upper class within a society

PROTESTANT—member of any of the Christian churches that broke away from the Roman Catholic Church during the 1500s

REFORMATION—religious change in which Protestant churches were set up in opposition to the teachings of the Roman Catholic Church

REGENT—person who is chosen to act as ruler of a country while the king or queen is absent, or is too young or ill to rule

STUART—family name of kings and queens of Scotland, including Mary, Queen of Scots. The Stuarts ruled England and Scotland after 1603

TRAITOR—someone who betrays or harms the leader or monarch of their own country

TUDOR—family name of kings and queens of England who ruled between 1485 and 1603, from Henry VII to Elizabeth I

TIMELINE

1513

Battle of Flodden and death of Scotland's King James IV

1533

Birth of Queen Elizabeth I of England

1542

8 Dec: Mary, Queen of Scots is born at Linlithgow, Scotland, the daughter of King James V and Mary of Guise

14 Dec: James V dies, leaving his baby daughter to be queen

1544

Henry VIII begins military campaign in Scotland to force marriage between Mary, Queen of Scots and Henry's son, Edward

1547

28 Jan: Henry VIII dies

10 Sep: English army defeats Scottish forces at Battle of Pinkie

1566

9 Mar: Murder of Mary's secretary, David Riccio

19 June: Prince James, later King of Scotland and England, is born in Edinburgh

1567

10 Feb: Lord Darnley is killed at Kirk o' Field, Edinburgh

Apr: Lord Bothwell is cleared of Darnley's murder. A few days later, Bothwell abducts Queen Mary

15 May: Mary marries Earl of Bothwell

24 July: Mary, imprisoned in Lochleven Castle, is forced to abdicate

1568

May: Mary escapes from Lochleven Castle but her forces are defeated at Battle of Langside

16 May: Mary flees from Scotland in a small boat, landing at Workington, Cumbria

Oct: Inquiry opens into whether Mary knew about or planned the murder of Darnley

1548

18 Aug: Mary, Queen of Scots travels to France to grow up at the French royal court

1558

Mary marries Francis, heir to the French throne. Elizabeth I becomes Queen of England

1559

Mary becomes Queen of France when her husband is crowned as King Francis II

1560

June: Death of Mary, Queen of Scots' mother, Mary of Guise

Dec: Death of Mary's husband, Francis II. Protestant religion is established in Scotland during the Scottish Reformation

1561

Aug: Mary returns to Scotland, arriving at the port of Leith

1565

July: Mary marries Henry, Lord Darnley

1569

Duke of Norfolk plans to marry Mary to challenge power of Elizabeth's ministers. Northern Uprising against Elizabeth

1570

The Pope excommunicates, or expels, Queen Elizabeth from the Catholic Church, giving Catholics the right to depose her

1571

Discovery of the Ridolphi Plot to assassinate Queen Elizabeth and replace her with Mary, Queen of Scots

1586

Discovery of the Babington Plot and Mary's coded letters to Anthony Babington

14 Oct: Mary's trial begins at Fotheringhay Castle

1587

8 Feb: Execution of Mary, Queen of Scots at Fotheringhay Castle

1603

24 Mar: Death of Elizabeth I. James VI of Scotland becomes King James I of England as well

SELECT BIBLIOGRAPHY

A Brief History of the Tudor Age, Jasper Ridley (Robinson, 2002)

A History of Britain Volume 1: At the Edge of the World? 5000 BC –AD 1605, Simon Schama (BBC Worldwide, 2000)

BBC website: "Elizabeth's Spy Network", Alexandra Briscoe **www.bbc.co.uk/history/british/tudors/spying_01.shtml**

Crown of Thistles: The Fatal Inheritance of Mary, Queen of Scots, Linda Porter (Macmillan, 2013)

Education Scotland website: Scotland's history **www.educationscotland.gov.uk/scotlandshistory/index.asp**

Elizabeth the Queen, Alison Weir (Pimlico, 1998)

My Heart Is My Own: The Life of Mary, Queen of Scots, John Guy (Fourth Estate, 2014)

Oxford Illustrated History of Tudor and Stuart Britain, John Morrill (ed.) (Oxford University Press, 1996)

WEBSITES

http://www.bbc.co.uk/timelines/zxnbr82
This BBC website tells the story of how the Tudors shaped modern Britain.

www.educationscotland.gov.uk/scotlandshistory/ renaissancereformation/index.asp
Education Scotland's web resources on Scotland's history include the story of Mary, Queen of Scots.

www.nationalarchives.gov.uk/spies/ciphers/default.htm
The National Archives website uses real documents to tell the story of Mary and the use of codes and ciphers.

FURTHER READING

Discover the Tudors: Elizabeth I, Moira Butterfield (Franklin Watts, 2014)

My Story: Mary, Queen of Scots, Kathryn Lasky (Scholastic, 2014)

The Fact or Fiction Behind the Tudors (Truth or Busted), Kay Barnham (Wayland, 2014)

A PERSPECTIVES FLIP BOOK

The Split History of

QUEEN ELIZABETH I
AND
MARY, QUEEN OF SCOTS

MARY QUEEN OF SCOTS' PERSPECTIVE

BY NICK HUNTER

CONTENT CONSULTANT:
Dr William Hepburn,
Teaching Assistant at the University of the Highlands and Islands
and Graduate Teaching Assistant at the University of Glasgow

raintree

a Capstone company — publishers for children

ABOUT THE AUTHOR:

Nick Hunter grew up in East Anglia. He studied history at the University of St Andrews and spent many years as a publisher of children's non-fiction books before becoming a writer. He writes about history and many other subjects, enjoying the challenge and responsibility of inspiring young readers and explaining the world to them. Nick lives in Oxford with his wife and two sons.

SOURCE NOTES:

Queen Elizabeth I's perspective

Page 4, line 2: The Stuarts spelled their name Stewart in the 1500s, but we've opted to stick with the more commonly used spelling for the purposes of this book.

Page 15, line 13 (p.186); page 18, line 17 (pp. 198–199): *Elizabeth the Queen*, Alison Weir (Pimlico, 1998)

Page 20, line 7 (p.565); page 20, line 13 (p.568); page 25, caption (p.581): *A History of Britain Volume 1: At the Edge of the World? 3000 bc–ad 1603*, Simon Schama (BBC Worldwide, 2000)

Page 21, panel, line 7: BBC website "Elizabeth's Spy Network", Alexandra Briscoe www.bbc.co.uk/history/british/tudors/spying_01.shtml

Page 23, line 12: Education Scotland website "Scotland's History", http://www.educationscotland.gov.uk/scotlandshistory/renaissancereformation/babingtonplot/index.asp

Page 27, panel, line 8: "The execution of Mary, Queen of Scots, 1587 Letters – Primary Sources", Marilee Hanson, from English History website, http://englishhistory.net/tudor/execution-mary-queen-scots-1587-letters/

Mary, Queen of Scots' perspective

Page 7, line 4 (p.14); page 11, panel, line 7 (p.155); page 12, caption, line 5 (p.194): All population figures from *My Heart is My Own: The Life of Mary, Queen of Scots*, John Guy (4th Estate, 2014)

Page 8, line 7 (p.552); Page 8, line 21 (p.554); page 14, line 11 (p.422); page 21, panel, line 7 (p.460): *Crown of Thistles: The Fatal Inheritance of Mary, Queen of Scots*, Linda Porter (Macmillan, 2013)

Page 8, line 14; page 24, line 11: Education Scotland website "Scotland's History", www.educationscotland.gov.uk/scotlandshistory/renaissancereformation/france/index.asp

Page 15, line 1 (p.556); page 16, line 14 (p.557): Schama

Page 25, panel, line 6: Education Scotland website, "Scotland's History", http://www.educationscotland.gov.uk/scotlandshistory/unioncrownsparliaments/jamesviandi/index.asp

Page 28, line 1 (p.569); page 28, panel, line 5 (p.579): Weir

Contents

CHAPTER 1

SCOTLAND AND ENGLAND

Mary Stuart was one of the great tragic figures of Scottish history.

When she returned to Scotland in 1561 after growing up at the French court, the young queen was renowned for her beauty and culture.

But being Queen of Scotland was very different from her situation in France. Mary would need courage and wisdom if she was to survive among Scotland's feuding barons. She would also have to deal with the competing attempts of England and France to win control of Scotland.

England's kings and queens had bullied their northern neighbour Scotland for centuries. After many decades of war, a treaty of 1328 made Scotland independent of England. But that did not stop the English interfering in Scotland's business.

Scotland's problems with the Tudor monarchs of England started when Henry VII seized the English throne in 1485. Henry and Scotland's King James IV fell out when James supported Perkin Warbeck, who claimed to be the rightful King of England. To try and build peace between the two countries, James IV agreed to marry Henry's eldest daughter, Margaret Tudor. Margaret was the sister of King Henry VIII, who became king in 1509.

CHILDHOOD OF A QUEEN

Mary became Queen of Scotland as a baby, but she was well aware of her own importance. In 1554, when she was just 12 years old, Mary had her own royal household where she would meet official visitors from foreign countries. She was renowned for her beauty and was able to spend a small fortune on clothes and jewellery. Mary was skilled at embroidery and music, and also loved outdoor sports.

The young queen had all the accomplishments of a French princess, but would the French help her to rule in Scotland?

PROTESTANT REFORMATION

There were problems in Catholic Scotland, too. Protestant ideas were sweeping across Europe in a movement called the Reformation. Mary's mother, Mary of Guise, had allowed some Protestant worship but when Protestants started attacking Catholic churches, she was forced to act. As she gathered her forces, the Protestant Lords of the Congregation raised their own army and marched on the capital, Edinburgh.

In 1558, England had a new queen. Elizabeth I was the youngest daughter of Henry VIII and a cousin of Mary, Queen of Scots. Mary's grandmother Margaret Tudor was Elizabeth's aunt. Elizabeth was Protestant and the Lords of the Congregation asked her for help against Mary of Guise's French forces. Scotland became a battleground for England and France. At the height of the crisis, in June 1560, Mary of Guise died.

LEAVING HOME

When Mary travelled to Scotland, her fleet included 12 ships to carry the queen, her household and all her furniture, clothes and jewellery. As the fleet left harbour, Mary looked back towards France and wept, saying, "It's all over now. Adieu France, I think I'll never see your shores again."

In just over a year, Mary had become Queen of France. She had lost her mother and husband. She now faced the challenge of returning to the religious turmoil of her homeland. She also had to deal with her hostile cousin Queen Elizabeth I. Elizabeth would not even allow Mary to travel through England on her way to Scotland.

Preacher John Knox was a leader in the Protestant Reformation. Knox's fiery sermons inspired Scottish Protestants to act.

MARRIAGE AND MURDER

lthough Mary disagreed with Queen Elizabeth on many counts, they had one important thing in common: they were women trying to rule alone in a man's world. Mary was the first queen to rule Scotland in her own right. She was only a teenager when she first landed in Scotland. Mary would be more able to control Scotland's quarrelling nobles if she had a husband to rule beside her. She also needed a child who would be her heir.

MAKING A GOOD MARRIAGE

There were many possible husbands for Mary among the royal families of Europe. She was not only beautiful and cultured, but anyone who married her would also gain control of Scotland. If she married Don Carlos of Spain, she would be making an alliance with the most powerful country in Europe. Neither the Protestant Scots nor the English would be happy with a partnership between Scotland and Catholic Spain. Queen Elizabeth wanted Mary to marry her favourite, Robert Dudley, but Mary was not keen.

She fell in love with Henry Stuart, Lord Darnley. This English aristocrat was handsome, clever and well connected. He was also related to the English royal family, which would make Mary's claim to the English throne even stronger. The couple married in 1565.

The young Lord Darnley was renowned for his good looks, although he was also dismissed as "being more like a woman than a man". This was not meant as a compliment.

Mary soon realized that Darnley was not as perfect as he first appeared. He was not ready to give up the single life of hunting and partying. He also found the job of governing a bit too much like hard work. The couple soon started to drift apart.

While Darnley was off having fun, Mary had to govern Scotland. She ruled from the Palace of Holyroodhouse with a small group of advisers. One of her most valued assistants was her Italian secretary, David Riccio.

MURDER AT HOLYROOD

Riccio controlled which of Scotland's restless lords could see the queen. The lords were unhappy about this. They started to spread rumours that the queen and Riccio were plotting behind their backs. Maybe they were planning to bring back the Catholic faith. The rebellious nobles also whispered to Darnley that he should have more control over his wife. After all, he was the king, wasn't he? Maybe the queen was fonder of Riccio than she was of Darnley, they hinted.

Darnley was convinced. He thought it was time his wife started listening to him, and Riccio was getting in the way. On 9 March 1566, Mary was dining with a group of friends, including Riccio, when the conspirators burst into the room. The queen, who was pregnant at the time, was powerless to stop them as they seized Riccio. Mary herself was even threatened before Riccio was brutally murdered.

Mary was terrified. She feared that she and her unborn child might be the next victims of the plotters. Despite her terror, Mary reacted calmly. She could see that Darnley was the weak link in the plot. She pretended to be ill and did everything she could to get him on her side. Together they fled Edinburgh to find safety in the castle at nearby Dunbar.

Mary raised an army and returned to Edinburgh in triumph. On 19 June 1566, she gave birth to a healthy son, James. Now there was an heir to the Scottish throne and Mary could turn her attention to the plotters.

EDINBURGH EXPLOSION

At around 2 a.m. on 10 February 1567, a massive explosion woke the people of Edinburgh. Lord Darnley, the queen's husband, was staying in Kirk o' Field, to the south of the city. The blast totally destroyed the house he was staying in, and it was no accident.

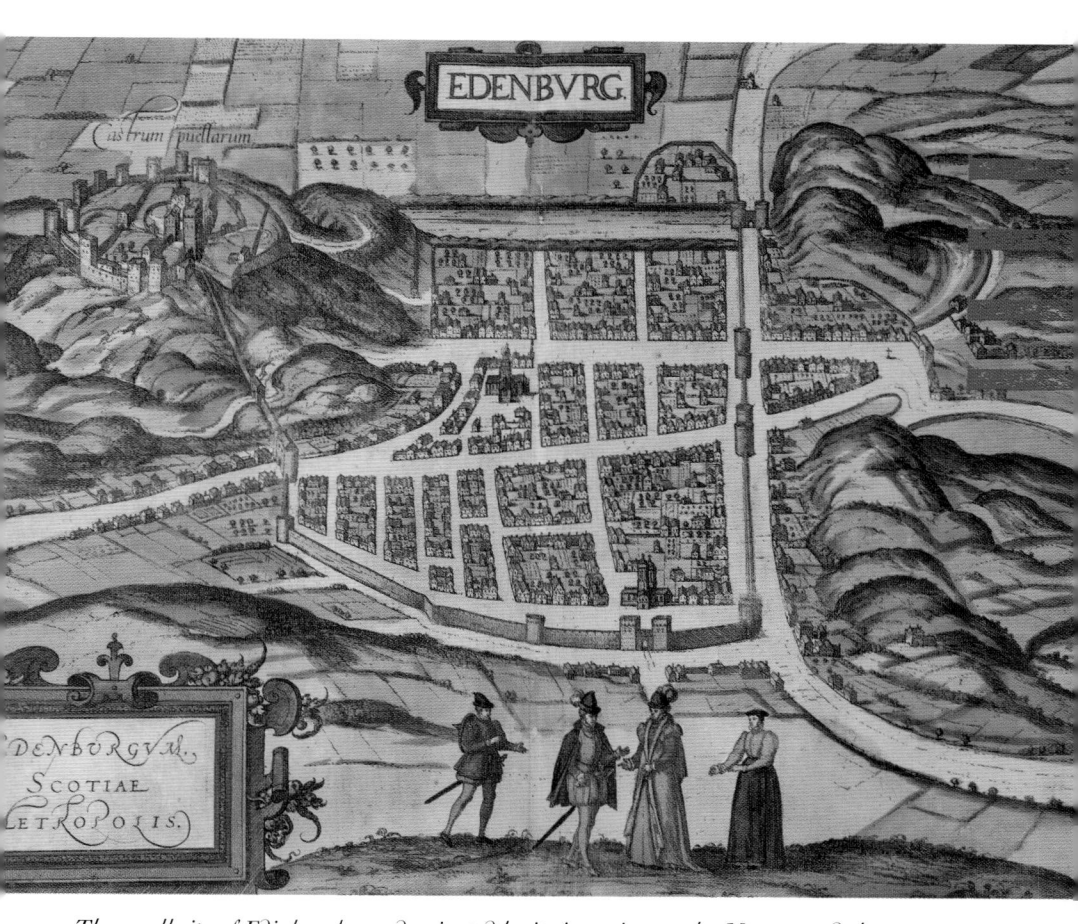

The small city of Edinburgh was dominated by its imposing castle. Mary moved there for her safety after the murders of Riccio and Darnley.

Darnley had been ill and Mary had suggested he should recover away from Holyroodhouse, so there was no risk to the health of their son, James. She had visited him earlier in the evening. The cellar beneath the house had been packed with explosives. The mystery deepened when Darnley's body was later found. He had not died in the explosion but had been strangled.

Everyone knew that Darnley had been murdered, but who killed him and was the queen involved?

The prime suspect was James Hepburn, Earl of Bothwell. He was one of the toughest and most ruthless nobles in Scotland and had been a loyal supporter of Mary. Bothwell was the only man to face trial for the murder. He was found not guilty but this may have had something to do with his armed supporters surrounding the court. Other plotters were probably also involved in the murder.

MARRIAGE TO BOTHWELL

Mary seemed to confirm that she supported and even helped plan Darnley's murder when she married Bothwell three months later. He had been loyal to her and opposed the lords who had attacked Mary's secretary. But Mary's marriage to Bothwell was not all that it seemed.

The queen was dismayed and unwell after the shock of Darnley's death. Bothwell saw his chance to seize power, and if Mary would not help him willingly, he would use force.

Mary turned to the Earl of Bothwell after Darnley's murder.

KIDNAP

Bothwell managed to persuade many of Scotland's lords and bishops
to sign a document urging Mary to marry him so that Scotland
would have strong leadership. Mary refused, but Bothwell was
determined to get what he wanted. On 23 April, he kidnapped Mary
and took her to Dunbar Castle. She would not be able to leave until
she agreed to marry him.

MARY ON THE RUN

When Mary, Queen of Scots married the Earl of Bothwell on 15 May 1567, she exposed herself to criticism. Protestant lords were quick to point out the supposed crimes of Mary and Bothwell. Mary would now have to fight for her throne.

Mary and her new husband faced a rebel army at Carberry Hill, but many of Bothwell's soldiers fled before the fight and Mary was captured. She returned to Edinburgh where the crowds had greeted her just a few years before. Now they turned on their queen, believing that she had plotted with Bothwell to murder her own husband.

Mary was taken to Lochleven Castle, which was surrounded by a lake. While there, she was forced to abdicate the throne and her baby son, James, became King of Scotland. Until James was old enough to rule, power would pass to Mary's half-brother, the Earl of Moray. Mary, who had been through so much, still believed that she could recover and prove her innocence. She sent messages to her supporters and started to plan her escape. On 2 May 1568, the castle-owner's sons, George and Willie Douglas, helped Mary escape by boat.

Mary still had a lot of supporters across Scotland. Many people knew the truth about her forced marriage to Bothwell, and many more wanted to defeat the Earl of Moray. Mary challenged him to return her throne. When he refused, Mary had enough support to raise an army. The two sides met at Langside, near Glasgow. Mary's supporters actually had more soldiers than Moray, but could not gain the victory that Mary needed.

George and Willie Douglas helped Mary escape by stealing the castle keys and rowing to safety across the loch.

Mary watched the defeat at the Battle of Langside from a nearby hill. She was running out of options. If she surrendered to Moray, she would certainly end up in a worse prison than before and with no chance of escape. There was even the prospect that Moray would execute her so that she could never again threaten his power. The only option that might save her was to seek help from her cousin, Queen Elizabeth I.

The small boat that carried Mary to England was very different from the fleet of ships that had brought her to Scotland a few years earlier.

The two cousins had had their differences, but surely Elizabeth would not stand by while a fellow queen, and family member, was forced from her throne?

Mary's supporters urged her to stay and fight. She still had enough support. Maybe she was weary of the constant struggle with the warring clans of Scotland, or maybe she really believed that Elizabeth would help her, but Mary had decided that her future lay in England.

Mary evaded capture and sheltered in a supporter's home near Dumfries, close to the English border. On 18 May 1568, she set out on her journey to England in a small boat. Her hair was cut short and she wore the simplest of clothes as a disguise. Mary, Queen of Scots would never see her homeland again.

DESPERATE ESCAPE

Mary later wrote of her desperate escape to England:

"I have endured injuries, … imprisonment, cold, heat, flight … and then I have had to sleep on the ground and drink sour milk and eat oatmeal without bread and have been three nights like the owls."

CHAPTER 3 YEARS IN CAPTIVITY

*M*ary did not expect to stay in England for long. Her escape would give her time to rally her forces against those who had taken her throne. Surely Elizabeth would help her. However, it was not long before Mary realized that she had made a terrible mistake.

When she arrived at Workington, in north-west England, Mary sent an urgent message to Elizabeth asking for protection. The local authorities took Mary to nearby Carlisle, where they could guard her until Elizabeth and her ministers decided what to do. A messenger would take several days to travel by horse from London so the answer was slow in coming.

The response was bad news for Mary. Elizabeth refused to see her because Mary was accused of murder. The Queen of Scots would stay in England as Elizabeth's guest, but she would be guarded and banned from moving freely around the country.

If Mary expected to be treated like a queen, she soon learned the truth. She had asked Elizabeth to send clothes fit for a queen in exile. What she received were the garments of an ordinary citizen.

PROVING HER INNOCENCE

Mary was angry and dismayed by Elizabeth's reply, and realized that she was now a prisoner in England. She wrote a letter insisting that she was innocent of Darnley's murder. She also stated that by refusing to meet with her, Elizabeth was encouraging Mary's enemies.

Mary's only hope of changing her situation came with the inquiry into her supposed crimes, which took place in 1568. Her hopes were dashed when the Earl of Moray produced the evidence that he said proved Mary's guilt – the Casket Letters.

The letters and various other documents had supposedly been discovered in a silver casket. Moray claimed that Mary had written the letters to Bothwell and that they proved she had known about and encouraged her husband's murder. Mary denied that the letters were in her handwriting, and she was never actually allowed to see them.

Mary spent her years of captivity in several different country houses, including Wingfield Manor in Derbyshire.

The letters, which no longer exist, were probably forged to provide supposed evidence of Mary's guilt, although many who saw them at the time were convinced she had written them. Mary refused to defend herself against the charges. In the end, the inquiry decided that there was not enough evidence to prove she was guilty, but that she could not return to Scotland.

Mary created this embroidery – known as the Marian Hanging – during her captivity.

SCOTLAND UNDER JAMES VI

In Scotland, there was growing support for Mary. In 1570, one of Mary's supporters assassinated the Earl of Moray. More conflict followed as the ruling lords tried to crush any support for Mary. From 1581, Mary's son King James VI was old enough to rule in his own right. He had been brought up as a Protestant and never saw his mother again after she left Scotland.

For years, Mary remained a captive in various country houses across England. She lived in comfort with a small community of servants. Her jailer, George Talbot, and his wife, Bess, closely watched over her. Mary spent much of her time doing embroidery, a common pastime for gentlewomen at the time. She also had opportunities to ride horses and hunt, but her freedoms stopped there.

Mary had fled to England to gain Elizabeth's protection rather than to plot against her. However, just by being in England she became a focus for Catholics who wanted a Catholic queen on the throne. Mary had two choices about how to deal with this attention.

If Mary ignored the plots against Elizabeth, she could not stop them happening and she might still be blamed. The only way that she would win her freedom could be with the end of Elizabeth's reign, or a successful plot against her. Elizabeth's treatment of her cousin forced Mary to become her enemy. Mary was particularly angry when her son, James VI, signed a peace treaty with England in 1586. This was while Mary was still Elizabeth's captive.

CHAPTER 4
TRIAL AND EXECUTION

In 1586, 18 years after she had arrived in England, Mary had some hope that her ordeal might finally be nearing its end. There were rumours that King Phillip II of Spain was preparing a great armada (fleet) of ships that would lead an invasion of England. The Catholic religion could be restored and Mary, Queen of Scots would be freed.

In May 1586, Mary sent two letters pledging her support for the proposed Spanish invasion. In return she heard news of a Catholic priest who was gathering support for a rebellion in England. Anthony Babington, a young Catholic supporter of Mary, was to lead the plot.

Babington wrote to Mary with details of the plot. He promised she would be Queen of England. On 17 July 1586, Mary wrote to Babington to give him her support for the plot to murder Elizabeth. Her assistants translated the letters into code and then she burned the originals. The coded letters were then smuggled out of her prison at Chartley Hall in empty beer barrels.

On 11 August 1586, Mary was out riding when she saw a group of men approaching. Were they her rescuers?

In fact, the men had come to arrest Mary. Elizabeth's chief spymaster, Francis Walsingham, had known about the plot from the start. He had recruited a Catholic double agent to intercept Mary's secret letters. Walsingham's agents had even come up with the idea of using beer barrels to conceal the letters.

SECRET CODES

Gilbert Curle, Mary's cipher secretary, wrote her messages in code. It was quite common at the time for important people to send messages in code in case they were intercepted. Unfortunately for Mary, the codes were not complex enough to outwit Walsingham's experts.

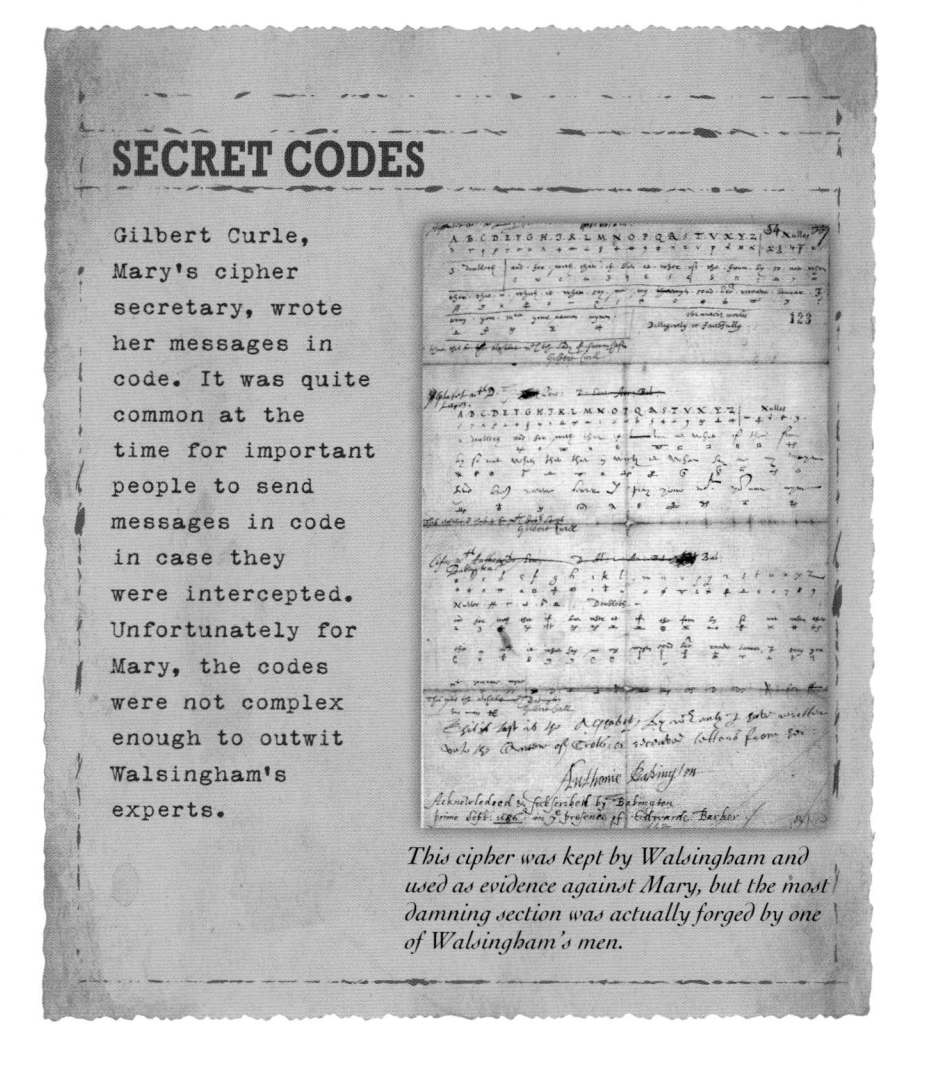

This cipher was kept by Walsingham and used as evidence against Mary, but the most damning section was actually forged by one of Walsingham's men.

ON TRIAL

Mary's trial began on 14 October 1586, by which time Babington and the other conspirators had already been executed.

Mary's first tactic was to claim that an English court could not judge her. She was Queen of Scotland and made the laws, although it was 20 years since she had reigned in her homeland.

When this failed, Mary claimed that she had no knowledge of the plot. This was difficult with all the evidence against her, but there was a possible loophole. Francis Walsingham had ordered that a small part of one of Mary's coded letters should be forged. Mary accused Walsingham of inventing the whole plot just so he could get rid of her. Mary said that she had only encouraged her supporters so that she could escape from prison.

Although she was right that Walsingham had forged at least one section of her coded letter, Mary was found guilty. Queen Elizabeth I would now decide her fate.

Mary discovered in November that the English Parliament had demanded a death sentence. After many months, Elizabeth finally agreed to the execution of her cousin.

A TROUBLED LIFE

On her last morning, Mary tried to encourage one of her servants with these words: "You have cause rather to joy than to mourn, for now you shall see Mary Stuart's troubles receive their long-expected end."

EXECUTION

At 8 a.m. on 8 February 1587, Mary faced her final ordeal in the Great Hall of Fotheringhay Castle. She removed her cloak to reveal her bright scarlet clothes – a colour associated with Catholic martyrs. After praying briefly, Mary was beheaded.

Mary, Queen of Scots is remembered not just for her tragic life. She made mistakes but she was also a victim of the conflict between Protestantism and Catholicism, the power struggle between England and Scotland, and the difficulties of ruling as a woman when men held almost all the power.

Mary showed no fear as she waited for the fateful moment of her execution.

INDEX